The Pledge

Cale Dietrich

FEIWEL AND FRIENDS
NEW YORK

To Jayden

A Feiwel and Friends Book
An imprint of Macmillan Publishing Group, LLC
120 Broadway, New York, NY 10271 • fiercereads.com

Our books may be purchased in bulk for promotional, educational, or business use. Please contact your local bookseller or the Macmillan Corporate and Premium Sales Department at (800) 221-7945 ext. 5442 or by email at MacmillanSpecialMarkets@macmillan.com.

Library of Congress Control Number: 2022033978

First edition, 2023
Book design by Mallory Grigg
Feiwel and Friends logo designed by Filomena Tuosto
Printed in the United States of America

ISBN 978-1-250-18697-3
10 9 8 7 6 5 4 3 2 1

Chapter One

TWO YEARS AGO

A meat cleaver goes through Sam's chest, killing him instantly.

"Damn it," he says as the bloody words GAME OVER splatter across the screen on his iPad. He unhooks his headphones and glances warily through the window in the door that leads outside to the deck and out to the forest. He stares at the darkness of the woods, and a wild thought of someone watching him invades his mind. He shivers.

He's sitting on a king-sized bed in a white tank top and boxers, with his legs stretched out in front of him. It's humid, and despite the best efforts of a fan in the corner of the room on the highest speed possible, he can't get comfortable.

He doesn't know why he can't relax. The only bad things that have happened on this weekend so far have been the man who stared at him and his boyfriend at the Pancake Barn before they got here, and Max's run-in with poison oak as they were walking back from the lake from their hike. Those can easily be explained: homophobia for the first, and Max's thickheadedness for the second. Everything else has been idyllic: the drive, passing by towering redwoods and Douglas firs, followed by a swim in Lake Priest, which Amy made sure everyone knew was actually a reservoir. Sam knows he has nothing to worry about, but he can't get rid of this grim feeling, no matter how much he tries to distract himself. Maybe playing horror games like *Hunting Ground* doesn't help, but he loves them too much not to. He does this a lot, watching scary movies or playing creepy games until he freaks himself out to the point where he can't sleep, picturing all the bad things that could happen to him. An ax murderer could burst through that door, or maybe this house is haunted by a demon that collects the souls of sixteen-year-old boys. Who knows?

Shaking off the thought, Sam opens his most recent Word document, where he has been editing his latest draft of *Tectonic*, a queer superhero novel he has been working on for the past year. He flips out the keyboard and starts to type. He's rewriting a big action scene, where Tectonic fights his archnemesis, the Grim Sailor, for the first time. Sam has a whole series mapped out in his head and has moments for books in the future that he already can't wait to write. And sure, maybe it's a little weird that he wants to follow in the same career path as his mom, but her being an author isn't why he wants to be one, he knows that. Ever since he was a kid, he has loved writing more than basically anything. And besides, his mom writes thrillers, and he wants to write about gay superheroes. They're different enough that he doubts anyone would be able to cry nepotism.

Outside, a floorboard creaks.

Sam's eyes flash to the door, where a figure stands. Cold washes over him. Then the figure steps into the light of his room and Sam scowls.

"Dude!" he says. "The hell is wrong with you?"

He locks his iPad, then crosses the room to the door, the soles of his bare feet padding against the thin rug atop the hard timber floor.

The boy standing outside, Eli, shoves his hands into his pockets and smiles. Even though it's hot as hell out, he always wears tight jeans.

"Where should I start?" says Eli.

They both pause.

Eli steps closer. He's incredibly slim and has cute, elfin features, including uneven ears that jut out and are pierced with black studs. His skin is only a shade or two darker than his skull-white tank, clashing with his cheaply dyed black hair, which he wears long enough to cover his eyes. Most people who meet Eli see this whole look, with the piercings and ripped clothes, and think he's going to be trouble, but Sam knows he's a sweetheart. He just thinks people who dress to blend in are boring. Plus, Sam thinks tank tops and ripped jeans are hot.

"Where are Max and Amy?" asks Sam.

"They called it a night. And then there were two."

Sam feels a smile tug at his lips. Energy builds between the boys, something chaotic and sparkling. Sam likes Eli so much: He likes how bitingly funny he can be, and how charming. Sam's heart starts pounding, his breaths get quicker. He's relieved that even after dating for this long, he still feels like this. On paper they aren't a couple that makes sense—semipopular nerd and emo guitarist isn't a combo either have heard of, but when the chemistry feels like *this*, like they're the only two people in the world right now, none of that matters.

"I have a surprise for you," says Eli. "Give me ten minutes, then come outside, okay?"

"What kind of surprise?"

"You'll find out in ten minutes."

Sam glowers. Eli kisses Sam on the cheek, then pulls a face.

"What?" asks Sam.

"Nothing."

Eli wrinkles his nose.

"I'll take a shower," says Sam.

"Good call. Ten minutes, okay?"

"Fine."

Eli turns and goes back across the deck. Sam grabs his phone from where it was charging on the bedside table and sets a countdown timer for ten minutes. Holding his phone, he goes through the quiet cabin, crossing a hallway that looks out at a combined kitchen and dining room. This lake house is usually rented out by Eli's parents on Getaway, and they charge $290 a night for people to stay here. Trying to get a reservation earlier than two months in advance is completely impossible. It's easy to see why: The cabin is gorgeous and modern, with off-white walls and plenty of tall windows that look out into the magnificent forest that surrounds Lake Priest. He goes into the bathroom, locks the door, and puts his phone on the sink.

Nine minutes and ten seconds to go.

He undresses and steps into the shower. He smells under his arm and scowls. It's not body odor, thankfully—but he definitely still smells like lake water. He pumps out some shower gel and rubs it into his armpits. He tilts his head back and lets the water run over his short black hair.

Once he's washed and conditioned his hair, he steps out and checks his phone.

Six minutes and three seconds.

He wraps a towel around his waist and goes back out. He stops. The front door is wide open. Was it like that before? He can't be sure, but he feels as if he would've noticed it if it was.

"Eli?" he asks, gripping his towel tighter.

He advances toward the door, taking slow, careful steps. Surely Eli wouldn't have left the door wide open like that. But then again, maybe he left it only slightly ajar and the wind pushed it the rest of the way open. Sam closes the door, then turns the latch to lock it. He goes completely still, listening, but he can't hear anything out of the ordinary.

He checks his phone again.

Five minutes and twenty seconds.

He goes back to the room he's sharing with Eli and tosses his phone onto the bed. He picks out a fresh shirt and a pair of shorts, as well as his favorite pair of underwear, and gets dressed, completing the outfit with a pair of sneakers. Once he's dressed, he goes over to the freestanding mirror on the other side of the room and starts pushing his hair into place. Normally he would use product to style it, but he figures he's on vacation, it's fine.

"Hey, Google," says Sam. "Play 'My Iron Heart' by Miss Vincent."

It starts to play from a speaker on the dresser.

Sam smiles and thinks back to the moment this trip was first planned.

"So," said Eli. "You know how I told you about my parents' lake house?"

"Yeah?"

"There was a cancellation, and Mom and Dad said we can take it as long as Max comes, too."

"Holy shit."

"Right?"

Sam opened his locker and put back his books.

"I've told you there's a hot tub, haven't I?" said Eli.

"Good thing I've been working out."

Sam flexed his arms, which made Eli laugh.

"You're such a douche," said Eli.

"Aw."

"Sorry, I can't help it. You're going to look mucho sexy in your trunks."

Eli got a C on his last Spanish quiz.

Sam moved Eli into a corner behind the locker, putting his hands on Eli's slim stomach. His fingers trailed across Eli's skin to his hips. "I can't wait," said Sam as he leaned in close to kiss his boyfriend, not caring who saw him.

Sam dances around the room, continually glancing at his phone. "My Iron Heart" is his favorite song at the moment, yet his brain is stuck on the door. Why did Eli leave it wide open? Or is someone else in the house with him?

The timer goes off, making him jump.

He grabs his keys and pockets them before going out through the door to the deck.

On the deck is a flickering tea candle. Another one is farther down, at the top of the stairs that lead to the bottom level of the house and the backyard. Sam smiles as he locks the door behind him. He picks up the first candle and blows it out, then continues on to the next one. He blows that one out, too, because these are cute but also a major fire hazard. He reaches the bottom level of the house. He was expecting a trail of tea lights to lead to the hot tub, and he was hoping he'd find Eli there, maybe with champagne, but the tub is quiet and dark. The trail of tea lights goes across the backyard, leading into the woods. The very dark woods. The air smells fresh and crisp, like the pine trees. Sam thinks it's funny that even a forty-minute drive away from the city is enough to make the air smell so much healthier.

Sam stops. He wishes now that he hadn't played so much *Hunting Ground* tonight. That was for sure a mistake. But Eli is out there, so how scary can it be, really?

He follows the tea lights into the woods, deeper and deeper. The temperature drops, and Sam starts to feel his heart racing. Normally he loves Eli's big gestures like this, but right now he would seriously love to be back in their room, with doors that lock.

He rounds a corner and sees Eli's plan. He has found a small clearing and is lying on a picnic rug, surrounded by small candles. But something is . . . wrong. Eli is slumped at an unnatural angle, facedown. Sam rushes up to Eli and rolls him over. He freezes at the sight.

Eli's entire chest is covered in blood. The material of

his tank top is soaked with red, and Sam catches a metallic smell. There's a deep gash on Eli's stomach, surrounded by dark blood. Sam feels panic rising, making him feel little more than an animal.

"Sam," says Eli, his voice croaky. "The man. He . . ."

Eli's face contorts with pain.

"Who?" asks Sam.

Eli closes his eyes.

Sam's instincts kick in, with every thought obliterated by the desire to run. Sam wraps Eli's arm around his shoulder and pulls his boyfriend to his feet. Eli can barely stand, but Sam is strong from his years of playing lacrosse. He can do this. A voice in the back of his mind tells him that he shouldn't move Eli, not with a wound like this, but he doesn't think he has a choice. If someone in these woods attacked Eli, then he needs to get him the fuck out of here.

He carries Eli back to the cabin and unlocks the front door. The pair rush inside, and Sam helps Eli to the couch and lowers him down as carefully as he can. Sam sprints back and locks the front door. He peers out through the high glass windows that look out at the forest, but he can't see anything. Eli shudders and coughs up dark blood. It trickles down his chin.

Sam forces himself to be calm. He thinks it through, and he knows what he needs to do. He takes out his phone and dials 911.

“Hello, what’s your emergency?”

“My boyfriend . . . I think he was stabbed.”

“Okay, where is he?”

“He’s . . . He’s here. He’s on the couch . . .”

“Sir, I need to know your address.”

“Shit. It’s . . . uh, twenty-three? No . . . thirty-two. Fuck! Eli? Eli, what’s the address again?”

“Twenty-three,” whispers Eli.

Sam says the address to the operator.

“Where was he stabbed?” they ask.

“His stomach.”

“Okay. An ambulance is on the way. Can you find a towel and put some pressure on the wound?”

Across the house, a scream sounds, coming from the second bedroom, where Max and Amy are sleeping. Sam’s mind wails with pure, overwhelming terror. Furniture crashes over, then something heavy is slammed up against a wall.

“No,” says Max. “Please—”

His voice is cut off, replaced by a sickening gurgle. There’s a wet sound, and then another crash of something hitting the floor.

“He’s here,” whispers Sam to the operator.

“Stay calm. Is there somewhere you can hide? If there is, go there right now.”

“Sam,” says Eli. “Go, save yourself.”

Sam gets up and runs to the kitchen. He grabs a knife from a rack on the counter, then goes back to Eli. He sets his phone on speaker and puts it on the coffee table. He stands at the ready, waiting for the attacker to emerge from the bedroom, which has gone quiet.

He's not going to leave Eli to his fate.

Help is on the way. He just needs to buy time.

The bedroom door opens, and a figure wearing a black balaclava emerges. He's obviously a man: He's got a large, masculine frame, covered in all-black clothes. In his hand is a serrated hunting knife, dripping with blood. Behind him, the bedroom is quiet.

Sam has never experienced anything like this: an overwhelming sense of wrongness coming from the man. This man is twisted. Broken. A freak.

"Stay back," says Sam as he raises his knife.

The man stops, seemingly amused. He wipes his knife on the front of his jacket, then takes a step forward.

"I said, stay back!" shouts Sam.

The man takes another step and switches the position of his knife. He charges forward, catching Sam by surprise. The man slices down, cutting Sam on the forearm. The cut burns. Sam turns and runs to the side. He almost makes it to the front door, but the man is too fast and swings with his knife. Sam ducks under it and makes a run for the other side of the house. He feels the man's fingertips grasp his shirt, and he pulls Sam back, then spins him around so Sam's back is up against the wall. The man stabs downward and Sam just catches his wrist, stopping the knife before it goes through his skull. Sam pushes him away so hard his muscles ache, fueled by a new burst of adrenaline. But he isn't strong enough. The man positions his knife and points it against Sam's heart, and starts to push in slowly.

Sam realizes he's about to die.

He will never see his family again. He will never get to become an author. He will never even see seventeen, all because this stranger . . .

No. Everything comes into focus. This isn't a stranger. There is only one person from his past who this could be. Shawn. The man who stalked Eli and made him transfer schools. This has to be him.

"Shawn," blurts Sam as it all comes into focus.

The man pauses, and Sam sees his chance.

He brings his knife up as hard as he can and stabs it right through the man's neck. The knife goes all the way through, so the end is poking out. Blood sprays all over Sam. The man, Shawn, staggers back. He falls to his knees, clawing at his throat; all the energy goes from his body, and he collapses, his body shuddering, a wet sound coming from his throat.

Sam lowers himself to the ground.

Blood starts to spread out around the man's body. He twitches and then goes completely still.

He's dead, realizes Sam. He killed him.

Darkness starts to close in.

He killed someone. He's a killer.

That's his last thought before his eyes close.

Someone shaking his shoulder pulls him back. There is a paramedic in front of him, with compassion in his eyes. Red and blue lights are visible through the front door. Sam shudders, because everything is coming back to him. Shawn is still where he fell but has been covered by a sheet.

Behind the pair, a stretcher holding a body covered by a sheet is pushed past. A pale hand hangs limply over the edge of the stretcher. Its fingernails are painted a pale pink. *Amy.*

"Eli," says Sam. His voice is rough. "Where is he?"

"The boy on the couch? They're looking after him now."

Sam tries to stand but just grimaces in pain and slumps back against the wall. Another stretcher is taken from the room, holding another sheet-covered body. Max, Sam figures.

"You're going to be okay," says the paramedic.

Sam just looks at him.

Okay?

Nothing is going to be okay ever again.

Chapter Two

TWO YEARS LATER

Killer.

I stare back at my reflection as that mental loop, the same word I've thought countless times these past two years, plays in my mind. There are dark circles under my eyes and black stubble on my cheeks. I've only just turned eighteen, but I think I could pass for thirty, if I had to. If I went anywhere, that is.

Killer.

Nobody I know has ever called me that, at least not to my face. And I know I shouldn't feel this way, and lately I only do on days of high stress. Like today. Shawn deserved it, at least that's what everyone I ask says. They've told me I had to do what I did that night. That it was self-defense, the only reasonable option. I had to kill, it was him or me, and I made the choice that any rational human being would make. Even my therapist, Dr. Patani, told me that I did what anyone would've done in that situation. As if that makes it okay.

They're wrong, though.

I *did* have a choice. A difficult one, sure, but it was still a choice. I held the knife. I chose to stab a man through the neck. No matter what he did, I made that choice. I chose to kill. I know I did the right thing, because I had to. Still, there's no denying it messed me up.

On my chest, by my heart, is a physical sign of the worst night of my life. It's a puckered, silvery-white scar, about an inch long. I have a longer one on my forearm. Up close, you can still see the marks on either side from the stitches. In the hospital, the nurses had to sedate me to close the wounds, because I was hysterical. I barely remember that, and when I do, I think of it like it's a movie I've seen or a book I've read. It's as if the past me is someone else. Sometimes I can't believe that really happened to me, even if it is what I think about all the time.

Sometimes thinking about why Shawn did what he did helps. He was a janitor at Eli's old school, and he had formed an unhealthy attachment to Eli. He started getting creepy, so Eli transferred schools, which was where I met him. It took a while for Eli to tell me about what happened. That same day, he said he was worried that Shawn would eventually find him. I was the one who talked him down, telling him multiple times that Shawn was a creep but not a threat anymore. I was wrong, and Shawn murdered Amy and Max and tried his best to kill Eli and me. He would've, too, if I hadn't done what I did.

A knock sounds on the bathroom door, making me jump.

"Is everything okay in there?" asks Dad through the door.

"Just a sec!"

I grab the pair of clippers that are resting on the sink. My hair is a long, shaggy mess, the black tips reaching my ears. Haircuts are one of the many things I stopped doing after the lake house. I couldn't trust anyone else to get that close to me with something sharp, not even my family. I tried once and had a panic attack. I turn the clippers on, and bring them up, and run them over my scalp. Thick clumps of hair drift around me, falling onto my bare shoulders. I run the clippers over again and again, until most of my hair is gone, leaving half an inch. I go over with the clippers one last time, evening it out.

There, done.

I'm a whole new man. The scruff needs to go, too, so I get started on that.

Once I'm done, I look cleaner and younger than I have in months. Maybe I only look a few years older than I really am now. I take off my boxers and step into the shower and turn the water on.

Killer.

No, no more. I've put myself through enough, and today is my chance to turn things around. Today is my opportunity to create a life for myself that might actually be worth living. They always say to fake it till you make it, and I figure that's worth a shot. After all, what have I got to lose? I tilt my head and let the water run over my face and then down over my scars. Sometimes I wonder about cosmetic procedures to get rid of them but always decide against it. My scars, like my past, are a part of me. Ugly, sure, but I can't change it.

I turn off the taps and step out of the shower. I wrap a towel around my waist and go out into the hallway. I wonder what Eli is up to today, and if I should message him. A few weeks after the lake, we decided to break up—I think spending time together reminded us of that night too much, and I, at least, wasn't in a place to be in a relationship. Sometimes I miss him so much it hurts, but I can't bring myself to message him. Every time I think about bringing him back into my life, I wonder what would happen if I can't handle it. I know it wouldn't be fair to get close just to withdraw again. I just hope that whatever he is doing, he's happy. He deserves that. I can hear everyone else downstairs, going about their morning routine. A Fleetwood Mac song is on right now, and I'll bet Dad is dancing along to it while he cooks breakfast. Peter will probably be around somewhere, but who cares where he is? Not me.

I reach my room and push my door shut behind me.

Even though I've lived here for nearly six months now,

this space—with walls the color of off milk and simple, minimalist furniture styled like an IKEA display—still feels much more like Peter's guest room than *my* room. Case in point: the painting of a boat that's above the headboard. I don't give a flying crap about boats, and I don't really respect anyone who does. I'd rather people flaunt their wealth in a way that's at least practical, and I'm not just saying that because Peter owns a yacht. Or maybe I am.

The only thing here that really feels mine is the column of four heavy-duty locks along the door. There are locks all over the house, on each of the doors and windows, and I make sure they're all locked before I have a shower or go to bed. Peter also bought the house the best home security money can buy, so there are little panels everywhere and security screens over each door that leads outside, and we've been assured that if anything happens, help will be here in minutes. Not that you always have minutes if you get attacked. We have taken every precaution, though, so maybe I should feel safe, but I don't: I honestly doubt I'll ever feel safe anywhere again. After someone tries to kill you, being safe is a notion that goes out the window.

There's an outfit resting on my bed: black T-shirt, indigo jeans, black Converse. Simple? Yes. But colors make me nauseous, and I think I look good in black.

I get dressed and go down to the kitchen. Dad is standing with his back to me, holding a knife. He brings it up and then brings it down, slicing off the head of the celery that he has on the chopping board. Knives still freak me out, but I know Dad would never hurt me. And yet I keep my distance. He slides the leafy end into the trash under the sink, then puts the stalks into the juicer to meet their doom, along with slices of apple, peeled orange wedges, and a hunk of ginger. Dad's gone through all the major food trends in the past two years: Thermomix, dehydrated fruits, acai everything, turmeric everything, and now he's landed back where he started, on smoothies and juices. A part of me is relieved I won't, for the time being, at least, have to try something made with kelp or something else gross. Talk about an unexpected perk of leaving for college. I probably won't be safe for long, though. Dad will find a way, I truly believe that.

I clear my throat, and Dad jumps. His skin is clear, and his short, reddish-brown beard is neatly trimmed. I have his blue eyes, but almost every other trait of mine I got from Mom. He's already dressed for work in a loose white shirt and relaxed khaki pants. Against his chest is a white crystal necklace, the one he always wears.

He turns around, and his eyes shoot up to my hair. Or my lack of hair.

"Looking good," he says, his face lighting up.

I scrub the back of my head with my hand. It feels prickly. "It's not too short?"

"Are you kidding? I love it. Now, stop fishing and help with the eggs."

Dad passes me a wooden spoon. Painfully bright early-morning sunlight streams in from the big windows above the sink, and a few fry pans are grilling breakfast food. It smells like bacon, so heaven. There are two pans, one vegan for Dad, and one regular for the rest of us. My stomach rumbles. I start folding the eggs over, gently scrambling them.

The kitchen, like the rest of the house, is airy and comfortable. Peter had it renovated last year, so now it has brand-new cabinets and white granite countertops to go with the white window frames, probably to try to impress Dad. Peter's basically wild about Dad, which I'd like if I liked Peter. Even this early, Dad's wearing his silver-and-onyx engagement ring. Not that I want to think about that. Hopefully it'll be a long, long engagement.

On a different pan, the bacon is crispy and browned, and there's a stack of toast beside me, the coating of butter already melted. My mouth starts to water, and my stomach practically screams at me to devour everything in sight like an animal.

"There he is!"

I grip the spoon I'm holding tighter.

Peter comes into the kitchen. He's wearing a navy polo with MARKET STREET DENTAL, the practice he owns and works at, stitched into the chest. He goes to kiss Dad on the cheek, so I look away before I can see the contact. Maybe I'm being immature. Actually, I know I am, but I can't help it. I know parents separate and find new partners all the time, and it's not like I don't get why things between Mom and Dad ended about a year and a half ago, about the time Mom got the book deal for *The Pleasant House*. My issue is that Dad is the best, and I don't think I'll ever understand why he picked *Peter* when he could have anyone. I mean, Peter's rich, sure, and money makes life a lot easier, but that doesn't explain why Dad is so moony. Peter doesn't like anything Dad likes, his main hobby is the giant train set he has in the basement, and his taste in TV shows is the worst: He only likes procedural crime shows or comedy shows with a laugh track. Plus, his teeth are too white. It's fucking creepy.

"Whatcha making?" asks Peter as he surveys the eggs.

"Tacos."

Peter chuckles, and Dad glowers.

"Good one," says Peter.

I'm pretty sure Peter has been counting down the days until today, when he finally doesn't have to deal with me, because I'll be at college and he won't have to put up with my shit anymore. I get it. I'm sure when he swiped right on Dad on Tinder, he didn't think he'd come with a son who has a metric fuck-ton of trauma. Imagine his bio: *Allan "Al"*

Carville, forty-three, currently a yoga instructor but not defined by work—I like reading and surfing and am newly obsessed with geocaching. Proud father to one normal kid and one survivor of the Lake Priest massacre, but you're not allowed to talk about it because it triggers him. Let's get coffee!

Peter looks down at his smartwatch, pulls a fake oh-shit-is-that-the-time face, and leaves to get ready for work.

As soon as he's gone, Dad turns to me and tilts his head to the side, his expression deadpan. Dad basically never gets mad at me, at least he hasn't since the lake house, but he *does* get disappointed, and that's somehow just as crushing. I guess we're still trying to find a middle ground, where he can stop walking on eggshells around me.

"What?" I ask.

His blank stare tells me exactly *what*.

"It's just the most obvious question," I say, gesturing at the food. "What does it look like we're making?"

"Be nice."

"Fine, sorry."

Dad watches me. "They should warn people about this."

"About what?"

"This." He gestures around the kitchen. "Like, sure, have a kid, it'll be great, but one day they'll leave for college."

"They should put it in the brochure."

He starts to tear up, and I probably would as well, if I had normal emotions still. They *are* there, but definitely less sharp than they used to be, which could be because of the antianxiety medication I'm on.

Honestly, without Dad I don't know if I would've made it to this point, where I am at least sort of ready to go out and face the real world. The first year after was *bad*: He saw me at my most unhinged, at my most anxious, and he never bailed. He brought food to my door when I couldn't leave my room; got me into therapy with Dr. Patani, which helped a lot; and talked me down the many, *many* times I cried. Mom tried her best, at least at the beginning, but she had a book to write and money to make, and it's obvious what she cares about more. She calls about once a week now, and she visited for a *very* awkward week last summer, but other than that, she's out of my life. I feel pretty shitty about it, but what are you going to do, you know?

I catch Dad watching me.

"What?"

He sits on the counter by the table and leans back. "Are you sure you don't want to take *one* writing class?"

I shake my head.

Dad doesn't get it. I wanted to be a writer when I was younger, sure, but I stopped a lot of things. I stopped playing lacrosse and seeing my friends and pretty much everything that made me, me. I'm a husk now, but I try not to be too hard on myself. Healing is a journey, and I'm taking it at my own pace. Maybe one day I'll want to write again, and I still think about *Tectonic* a lot, but I'm not there yet.

Dad has made it abundantly clear multiple times that he's disappointed I'm not going to go down the path of an artist, the one he didn't because he wanted to be practical—he used to sing and play ukulele in a folk band, and they got big enough that they played a few hippie festivals. But it was demanding and expensive, and touring would take him away from Mom. Then she got pregnant with me, so he took a marketing job working for his father, which he kept for years and which, in his words, crushed his soul. Finally he had enough and quit everything, which led to his new job as a yoga instructor.

I get why he's wary, but I don't want to go to college and get a degree and a whole bunch of debt and come out of it with the uncertain job prospects of an artist. No, it's clear that becoming a psychologist is the right plan for me—it has good pay and low unemployment, and I can help people, like Dr. Patani helped me. Hopefully I'll be okay with strangers by then.

"I just don't want you to regret it," he says.

"I won't."

He touches his pendant, like he always does when he's thinking hard. I'm a little annoyed, honestly. Like, yeah, it must suck to have given up on something he used to really want, but he and I aren't the same. And who knows, I could've grown out of wanting to be a writer even without Lake Priest. I did want to be a chef for years when I was a kid, after all, to the point that I used to cook all the time, making Mom and Dad sample my creations—one of which was pasta with a sauce made by mixing ketchup and mayo. To their credit, they ate it to encourage me, but still, I shudder at the memory.

"All right, I'll stop," says Dad as he sprinkles some chopped parsley from his garden onto the eggs. "Can you get Gus?"

I go upstairs to Gus's room and push open the door. He never closes it all the way. His room is still dark, the sunlight only peeking in under his blinds, and I can see him on the edge of his bed, wrapped up like a burrito.

"Hey, buddy," I say.

He shakes his head and wraps himself up tighter in his blanket. I go into his room, carefully moving around the Lego war that he currently has going on around the foot of his bed, complete with two opposing Lego dragons and a squad of ninjas riding quad bikes. I sit on the end of his bed and poke him in the stomach.

"I'm sleeping," he says, pulling his blanket over his head.

"Come on, I've got shit to do."

He sits up. Then he sees my hair, and his mouth drops open. "What did you do?"

"You don't like it?"

"Umm . . ."

"Gus!"

"What? It's just a lot. It's growing on me."

I give him a blank stare. "Nice save."

"Swear jar, by the way."

"I'll put ten dollars in if you get up right now."

He smiles. His black hair is too long and it's giving off an evil-scientist vibe as it's sticking out in all directions. People used to say all the time that we looked alike, even with a large age gap: We have the same facial structure, with dark hair and thick eyebrows inherited from Mom, and he has Dad's eyes, too. I wonder if anyone would say Gus and I look alike now. Probably not.

Seeing him, I want to stay. He's been changing so fast, and who even knows what he will be like the next time I see him? Will he still even like throwing Lego wars? Will he like haircuts all of a sudden? He surprises me all the time by how much of a proper person he's becoming. How much am I going to miss by making this decision?

"Sam," says Gus.

"Yeah, bud?"

"What if he comes back?"

I pause.

I remember the moment Shawn went still: the moment the fear passed, and I realized I was no longer in danger, and the full force of what I'd done hit me.

"He can't," I say. "He's gone."

I wish Gus didn't have to worry about this. Dad and I have tried our best to shield Gus from this side of our lives. I mean *our*, too—what happened has impacted all of us. Dad never used to carry pepper spray, and now he won't leave the house without it. As much as we've tried, Gus is smart, and he's figured it out even without us telling him the complete picture. He might not know all the gory details, but he knows enough to know we definitely aren't a normal family, and there is something very different about me especially.

I offer him my little finger. "I wouldn't go if he wasn't."

He folds his little finger around mine. Then he smiles and unwraps himself from his blanket, like a butterfly emerging from a cocoon. I get up and go back downstairs, feeling a dense weight pressing down on me, and stick a twenty-dollar bill from my wallet into Gus's jar. Dad has assembled a plate for me, loaded high with everything. Perfect. Peter comes back in and sits at the table, and he scrapes his knife on the plate, making a scratching noise.

I sit down opposite Peter and take a bite of the buttered toast he's handed me, flashing him a small smile.

I know I'm lucky that I made it out of there with just scars. It could've been so much worse, but . . . no. I'm not thinking about Shawn today. Today I'm starting afresh, and that means no thinking about him, or what I've done.

"How's work going?" I ask Peter, hoping to distract myself.

"Busy." Peter cuts into his piece of toast, and his knife scrapes the plate again, like he's trying to do it to get a rise out of me. "I was thinking last night, and I'm a little jealous of you."

Dad tenses. I don't even know what to say to something that's so mind-bogglingly stupid and insulting.

"College was the most fun I've ever had," continues Peter. "I'd love to go back."

"Grass is greener, I guess."

He chuckles, missing the dark tone in my voice, then returns to his breakfast. Dad is glaring at me, as upset as he ever gets at me. I mouth the word *sorry*, and then get back to eating. My stomach protests. I put my knife and fork down and instead take a big sip of my juice as Gus appears in the kitchen, dressed for school, with the Pikachu backpack I got him last Christmas slung over his shoulder. His hair is still a wild mess.

"Did you shower?" asks Dad.

"Yeah."

"Lie jar," he says, snapping his fingers and pointing.

Gus moans and shoves a dollar into his jar. We have one for each of our vices: me, swearing; Gus, lying; Dad, being late; and Peter, snoring—which I suspect is a joke, as it's the only jar with no money in it.

"Go," says Dad, pointing his knife upstairs. Gus rolls his eyes, then trudges back to the bathroom. I feel an ache inside my chest. This is my last morning here. After today, everything is going to change, and who knows if I actually am ready for this. I don't feel safe here, but I guess I feel somewhat okay, ready enough to branch out, at least.

This is just jitters talking. I'm ready. Dr. Patani has said so, she even said it would be a good thing for me. She thinks I'm ready to start integrating into society again. And I do agree with her. I've made really great progress, I think as much as it's possible while still spending most of my time in my bedroom. I'm not just telling myself this. I believe it.

I'm ready.

I slam the trunk of the car shut.

We've done some real *Tetris*-style packing, and now Dad's Jeep is filled with all my stuff. I've gone through the list I made six times, to make sure that I haven't forgotten anything. I want today to be perfect, down to every tiny detail. I have all my paperwork in my backpack, which is in the passenger seat, along with my laptop. My textbooks, which I bought online and were still ridiculously expensive, are in my suitcase.

Peter and Gus are standing on the lawn by the mailbox.

Peter's hand is on Gus's shoulder. Dad is at the wheel of his car, his pride and joy, aside from Gus and me. He's on the phone, talking to Grandma, already debriefing.

Peter sticks out his hand, and I shake it. Peter's grip is too tight, and it hurts.

"Have a great time," he says.

"I will."

I turn to Gus, and he throws his arms around me. My heart threatens to splinter. I crouch, so I'm eye level with him. Peter seems to know he's intruding, so he turns away. Tears well up in Gus's eyes.

"Look after Dad, okay?"

"He's supposed to look after me."

"I know. But can you?"

His mouth twitches. "I will."

I tousle his hair. "Good man."

Gus will be okay. It might be better for me not to be around him so much, so his life can be a little more normal. It can't be good for an eight-year-old to be around me all the time. I go around to climb into the passenger seat, then close the door behind me.

"Gotta go, Mom," says Dad. "Love you."

He hangs up, then turns to me. "Got everything? Phone, wallet, keys?"

I check my pockets, and I have everything. Including my Taser.

"Yep," I say.

Dad starts the engine. Peter still has his hand on Gus's shoulder, squeezing it tight.

I wave, and Dad pulls out of the driveway, onto the street.

There's no going back now.

Chapter Three

"Look," says Dad, pointing out the front window at a sign that says MUNROE UNIVERSITY—NEXT EXIT.

I pause the video I was watching on my phone, stopping Rock M. Sakura mid-sentence. She's one of my favorite drag queens, which is seriously saying something, because I hard-core love pretty much all of them. I've seen almost all the seasons of *Drag Race* multiple times, including all the international spin-offs and all-stars. What can I say? When you're homeschooled, have no friends, and don't leave the house, you have the time to watch *Drag Race* nonstop. If I'm not watching *Drag Race,* I'm probably watching a Marvel movie, even though I prefer DC characters, or playing Pokémon. I read online once that sticking to familiar media is a sign of anxiety, and I am pretty confident that is the case for me. I know *Drag Race,* Marvel movies, and Pokémon. The odds of them triggering me are extremely low.

We go past the sign.

"Cool," I say.

"That's your reaction?"

"It's a sign."

"It's exciting, Sam!" says Dad, jostling my leg with his free hand. "You're going to college!"

Up ahead, the campus starts coming into view. Oh damn, this is actually happening. I'm actually going through with this. It's such a turn for me, which in a lot of ways is the whole point. Dr. Patani is actually the one who nudged me toward this choice and told me that I'm ready to stop seeing her so much. I have an appointment booked in a few weeks, to check in, but she believes I can do this. She said she's always happy to see me if I need to talk, but she thinks that mentally, I'm strong enough to stop seeing her so often. A part of me thinks it might be smarter to keep seeing her, especially as my life is changing, but I trust her advice. Also, it's difficult to have a fresh start if I see her all the time.

Dad turns the radio up. "Cool for the Summer" is playing. I love this song, but nowhere near as much as Dad does. He starts lip-synching along, which brings up a lot of questions. First, when did he learn all the words? And second, why?

"Why?" I ask.

"I'm trying to hype you up!"

"I'm adequately hyped."

The chorus hits, and Dad starts banging his head along. I know he wants me to join in, and for this to be a moment, but dancing makes me uncomfortable. I turn in my seat and look out the window. There's a little guilt, sure, and I appreciate Dad for trying so hard, especially when Mom hasn't even messaged me, but I'm not lip-synching. I'll leave that for drag queens.

We pass by a bunch of large suburban mansions, most of which have expensive cars out front. The whole place looks clean, and rich, the houses all spectacularly designed, the streets pristine. Maybe students live in these houses—I don't know who would want to live this close to a campus if they weren't studying, and it doesn't seem like there's anything else too exciting out here. If there is, I haven't noticed it on this drive.

I roll down my window and rest my hand on the edge. I have this whole day planned out already in my head. I have all the steps memorized, and that makes it easier. All I have to do is go through the motions, and there won't be any curveballs, and I will have a perfect first day of school. It'll be easy, and that's what I want.

We turn a corner the GPS tells us to take, and I see it in the distance.

Munroe University.

It's as stunning as ever and looks even better than it did on the tour. The buildings are mostly a bright cream color, with reddish-brown tiles on the roofs. And it's so green: The lawns are bright and meticulously maintained. It's a weirdly hot day for September, and hot, dry air comes in through the window. I tend to get sick of the rain in winter, but it'd be preferable to this.

"Wow," says Dad.

"Right?"

"My college was a *dump* compared to this."

"Really?"

"It was like a prison. This is gorgeous."

We drive down the street and reach my dorm: Sorosiak Hall. It's a grand building, with a triangular reddish-brown tiled roof above the entrance and white Greek-style columns out front. It's not too far from the rest of the campus—I can see the library and a church, along with a few modern classroom buildings. On a grassy area to the left of the hall, a group of students are tossing a football to each other. One of the guys is really hot: a muscular jock in a tank top. Basic? Yes, but what can I say? I haven't been around a guy like that in a while, and I'd almost forgotten how magnetic they can be. He could toss me like that football if he wanted to.

Dad parks and turns off the engine. I'm glad he can't read my mind. Dad has always been cool with my sexuality after I came out at eleven, but that doesn't mean I want him knowing my exact thoughts about the jock over there.

"Ready?" asks Dad.

"Just need a sec."

I close my eyes and try to ground myself. I splay my hand and then clench it into a fist, digging my nails into my palm.

This is okay.

I deserve good things. I deserve to be happy.

But the truth is I deserve to be normal. I don't want to know what it feels like to take a life. And it's all so unfair.

"Panic attack?" asks Dad. "Talk to me."

"It's not a panic attack, I'm just . . ."

"What?"

"What if it gets bad again?"

"Then you come home and try again next year."

I look out the front window. Peter's place isn't home. Plus, I don't want to try again next year. I want this to work now. I don't want another year of making Dad's and Gus's lives revolve around me. They've had enough of that. They need space as much as I do.

"You're right," I say. "What have I got to lose?"

"Exactly," says Dad, and he puts his hand on his door handle.

I wipe my sweaty palms on my jeans and then get out of the car, grabbing my backpack and slinging it on before pushing the door shut. It's sweltering, even though it's not even nine thirty, and jeans were a mistake. The sky is crystal clear and a vivid, bright blue, and I don't even want to think about how hot it's going to get later in the day. Dad and I enter through a glass door. Inside is a large lobby area filled with students.

Dad and I go up to the receptionist.

"Checking in?" she asks.

"Yep."

"Do you have your paperwork?"

I pull it out of my backpack and hand it over.

"Excellent," she says as she starts entering the details into her computer. "Oh, single room, very nice."

"He insisted," says Dad.

I wince. I did insist. Just because I'm working on myself doesn't mean I want someone in my space all the time.

"There we go," says the receptionist, and she hands over a key card. "This'll get you into your room. Welcome to Sorosiak."

I take the card and put it in my wallet. "Thanks."

"Now," says Dad. "I've already called and been assured about this, but just to be completely safe, what's the security like here?"

She blinks a few times, as if totally surprised by the question. "Um, no one can get into the building after nine unless they swipe their key card. The campus has security guards at night, and there are always people walking around."

Dad doesn't seem convinced. "Thanks."

We move away from the desk.

I'm on the seventh floor, which I had to request because there was no way I was staying anywhere near ground level. Dad and I go down the hall. Each door has a whiteboard stuck to it, and a lot of people have already written their names on them, along with their interests. I now live near someone named Rick, who likes *Attack on Titan* and *The Wheel of Time*, apparently. He lives next door to someone called Jace, who likes football and MMA.

Dad and I find room 711, which matches the number on my key card. I scan my card and push the door open.

The room is actually pretty big. It's the size of a usual dorm room, only there's just one bed on the right side of the room, meaning there's a lot of extra space where a roommate's stuff should be. But still, the carpet looks new, and there's a big window in the far wall that overlooks the campus. Dad and I go over and look out. From here, I can see a brass statue in the middle of the quad of Marvin Munroe, the school's founder, and tiny figures walking around.

"Happy?" asks Dad.

"Yeah," I say.

"Come on, gimme more than that. This is amazing!"

"Yeah, okay, it is."

"We're going to decorate the shit out of this place. It's going to look so good."

In my pocket, my phone buzzes. I have a new message.

Have a good day today. ☺

I frown.

"You okay, kiddo?" asks Dad.

"Yeah . . . yeah, all good," I mumble as I type a message back.

Thanks Mom.

Chapter Four

I hang the last string of lights above my bed, and now I'm finally done decorating my room.

Have a good day today. ☺

Mom really went all out with her message. I know I was mad about her not even messaging before, but this doesn't feel like enough. Dad has done so much for me today, and she can't even be bothered to call. It's so typical of her, and yet it still hurts.

Dad is standing below me, assessing the work I've done. I've decorated the far wall with pictures of art I like. Even with all my stuff, the room still seems too big. Too empty. This whole time I've been decorating, I've been trying not to think about the message I got from Mom. If she really cared, she would've called.

"Happy?" asks Dad.

"So happy."

A knock sounds on my door. Before I can ask him to slow down, Dad goes over to the door and opens it. Outside is a boy. A gorgeous boy. He's tall and fit, wearing a tailored shirt tucked into his pants in pure, preppy perfection. His skin's a light shade of brown, and his hair is styled impeccably, short on the side leading to tight curls. Over his shoulder is a leather satchel bag, and he's gripping the strap tight with one hand.

"You must be Sam," he says, walking in and offering his hand. "I'm Oren, your RA."

"Hi." My voice kind of hitches, so I sound like I'm unsure of my own name. Abort, abort! "This is my Dad."

"Al," says Dad, as he sticks his hand out, then shakes Oren's hand. "Are you a senior?"

"Sophomore." Oren stands up straighter. "I lived here last year; it's great."

Oren walks inside and checks the place out. I glance at Dad, and he mouths the word *wow*.

"I love what you've done with the place," says Oren with an almost alarming level of sincerity. He tucks his hands into his armpits, and man, his arms are nice. Boys should be cute or hot, and Oren is a devastating combination of the two.

Okay, I've forgotten how to talk to cute boys. I've never really been good at it, but now it's especially bad. He's just so cute, and I . . . oh shit.

He has a rainbow bracelet on.

If I was nervous before, now it's especially bad. Because

holy shit, not only is Oren super cute, he's actually an option. This is dangerous.

"Thanks."

"I live just down the hall," says Oren, oblivious to the mental freak-out currently going on inside my head. "If you need help with anything, just let me know."

"Will do."

"Wait," says Dad, stopping Oren just before he leaves. "Are there any parties tonight?"

Oren raises an eyebrow. A perfect eyebrow.

"Not for me," blurts Dad. "For Sam."

I cross my arms, but I can't deny that I am curious. Even if it is absolutely mortifying that Dad is asking this, not me. It's like I'm five years old and he is trying to organize a playdate, which is definitely not what I want Oren to think of me.

"Well, my fraternity is having a rush thing tonight, if you're interested?"

Oren reaches into his pocket and pulls out his phone.

"What's your number? I can text you the details."

Be still, my heart. College was a good idea after all, if I can get a guy like Oren's number right way. I tell him my number, and a few moments later, my phone buzzes. He's linked me to an event called Alpha Phi Nu Rush.

"Come by the house and meet the guys," he says. "It's super chill."

"Sweet."

"Hopefully I'll see you there," says Oren, and he goes farther down the hall. Dad closes the door behind him, then his eyes fall on me, alarmingly knowing.

"Why are you looking at me like that?" I ask.

"Oh please, you're going."

"I'm not."

"Come on, you're seriously telling me that boy didn't do it for you?"

"I'm not talking about this."

"That's the spirit. Come on, he's cute."

"Shh."

Dad mimes zipping his lips shut. "Is there anything else you need?"

I've planned almost everything, so I already have all the things I'll need for the day my classes start.

"I wouldn't mind getting a Munroe hoodie," I say.

"In this weather?"

Dad's always on my case for often wearing winter clothes even when it's scorching out. I do get uncomfortable, but sometimes I don't want anyone to be able to see the scar on my forearm.

"For later."

It's part of my plan for the day: I've always envisioned getting a Munroe hoodie on my first day, as a sort of commemorative thing.

We leave my room, and I make sure the door locks properly behind me before Dad and I go down the stairwell.

"I think we're going to have to have a talk about using protection," says Dad, completely out of nowhere.

"Oh God."

"You know about condoms, right?"

"Yes."

"There's a pharmacy on campus. You can get them there."

"I know."

We make our way across the campus, and we go into the main quad building, which is three stories tall and is built in a wedge shape. There's a frozen yogurt store, a Chinese place, a 7-Eleven, and a sandwich place, which I suspect I will go to a lot, as long as it accepts my prepaid meal plan. Dad and I go into the Barnes & Noble.

The store is massive, split over two levels, with the downstairs area selling textbooks, while on the top there is a popular-fiction section to the right, but most of this level is selling supplies like pens and notebooks, along with countless racks of Munroe merch, proudly displaying the navy blue and deep red school colors.

I start to browse, looking at the hoodies. I find one and reach into it, and it's really freaking soft. I'm glad, because it costs forty bucks. I pick out a gray T-shirt with MUNROE across the chest and a dark red hoodie with PATRIOTS on it. Now that I'm happy, I go over to Dad, who is in the popular-fiction section, and oh no.

He's found Mom's book.

It's called *The Pleasant House*, and it has a simple cover: just a small house by a lake in front of a creepy smiling face graphic, with the title and Mom's name, Nina Carville, along the top, underneath the words *Based on a true story*. Yeah, mine. She didn't directly rip me off, but it was close enough. She just changed Sam Carville to Sara Chambers, and she made the killer wear a Halloween mask of a creepy smiling face, and boom: It's fiction.

Dad grips the cover and rips it off, before stuffing it back onto the shelf. I'd be upset if it were any other book, but seriously: Fuck that book.

"Got everything you need?" asks Dad.

"Yep."

Dad buys my new clothes, and then we head out and start walking back to my dorm. I realize what is happening right now: Dad's about to leave. Adrenaline starts to pump through my blood, but it's under control. I can handle this.

"Are you okay?" asks Dad.

"Yep."

Dad and I walk in silence back to the car. The yawning pit of anxiety spreads, making my head spin. *Don't panic. This is perfectly normal, and everything is perfectly fine. You have no reason to freak out.*

We reach his Jeep and stop in front of it.

"Are you sure you're all right?" he asks.

"Go, you're cramping my style."

"Please. If anything, you're cramping mine."

"Dream on, old man."

He steps forward and hugs me really tight. The moment he should've ended the hug comes, and then goes.

"What's wrong?" I ask.

"Nothing. I'm so proud of you." He clears his throat. "This suits you."

He gestures at me and the space around me. He stops because something has caught his eye. I look in his direction and see a completely naked guy running across the road. There are Greek letters painted across his chest. He seems like a surfer-type guy, as he has skin so tan he is almost orange, and his hair is sun-bleached blond.

"You don't see that every day," says Dad.

You certainly don't.

"One last hug?" asks Dad.

He grips me again. Then we break apart, and he gets into his Jeep. He closes his door and then lowers his window.

It's times like these that I hate Shawn more than ever. I will always hate him, but in a lot of ways he took this day from me. It's not how it should be. Sometimes I feel everyone in my life is acting, as if we're pretending more than actually living, because we both know what we're really thinking about, yet we can't bring it up, at least not directly. Dad shouldn't be worried that I'm going to have a mental breakdown being away from my safety net, and I shouldn't feel like I don't deserve this, because a normal person hasn't killed anyone. I should be nervous, but in an excited way, like everyone else here.

"Can you promise me one thing?" asks Dad. "Try to have fun."

"What's that?"

He laughs. "Join that frat. Kiss a boy. You deserve to live, Sam."

"Bye, Dad. Love you."

"Love you more."

With that, he turns on the engine. His eyes brim with tears. He waves again, then pulls out of the parking spot and then honks his horn a few times before driving away. I watch as the car goes around a corner, then goes out of sight.

Breathe, dude. Just breathe.

I go back inside the dorm. My room is empty and quiet.

I open the message Oren sent me about the fraternity and delete it.

Chapter Five

A loud thud sounds on the front door of the lake house.

A storm is raging outside, with crackles of lightning streaking across the sky, lighting up the room with brilliant white light. Rain pounds against the window. Through it, I can see trees being jostled by the storm. It's really bad out there, and I'm glad I'm inside, where it's warm and safe.

The thud sounds again, louder this time.

Beside me, Eli is fast asleep, his back turned away from me, his bare shoulders hunched. He's so slim I can see the bones of his spine. Like always when we share a bed, he's stolen all the blankets. Eli's the heaviest sleeper I've ever met; he can sleep through *anything*.

I sit up and look at Eli for a moment. He's so beautiful and at peace. I get out of bed, moving slowly so I don't wake him. The floor is cold against the bottoms of my feet.

I walk through the dark living room to the front door.

Shawn pounds his fist on the door again, so hard the whole door rattles. He starts hammering his fist against it, faster and faster. On a table by the door is the kitchen knife I used to kill, as if it's waiting there, just for me. I go past it, until I'm standing right in front of the door. Up close, I can see the detail: There are small flowers and birds etched into the wood.

The hammering stops.

Here it goes.

I open the door.

Shawn is standing on the porch, as I was expecting him to be. Drops of water have collected on his balaclava and on his black leather jacket. I'm rooted to the spot, frozen by fear. He's holding his hunting knife at his side.

His free hand shoots out, and he grabs me by the neck.

I raise my hands and try to pry his grip away from me, but he's holding too tightly, and there's nowhere I can go. Lightning streaks across the sky. He lifts me up off the ground, so my legs are dangling. My eyes threaten to bulge out of their sockets. There are two bloody slashes on his neck where my knife went in, and out. They're freshly bleeding, and the blood is seeping into his shirt.

BZZT.

I wake up and sit bolt upright. I'm totally disoriented, and that feeling quickly turns to panic. Where am I? This isn't my bed, this isn't my room—but then it dawns on me where I am. I'm in my dorm room. I chose to come here; I haven't been taken anywhere against my will. My phone is buzzing on my bedside table. The last thing I remember was lying down to listen to some music, and then I decided to have a nap, and that was a few hours ago. My headphones are still on. Outside, it's just starting to get dark, so I'd guess it's around six. The campus is a lot quieter now than it has been all day, and there are only a few small groups of people still outside, instead of the large crowd that I could see earlier in the day.

I grab my phone and swipe to answer the call.

"Hello?" I say.

"Hi," says Mom. "How are you?"

"Fine."

"Big plans tonight?"

I look around my quiet room. "Not really."

"What are you going to do?"

"Dunno."

"Is this a bad time?" she asks.

"No, what's up?"

"I want to know about your day."

"It was fine, nothing really exciting. I got a hoodie, decorated my dorm, braved the shower for the first time."

"That's good. You don't want to risk your recovery, do you?"

"No."

"You should take it slow; that's smart."

"Yeah, I know. How was your day?"

"It was okay. I made some good progress on my draft."

I grit my teeth. I don't want to hear about Mom's books.

About any of them. Not after she used my trauma for her own gain. In a way, I get why she did it, because her career had majorly stalled. Her debut thriller got heaps of attention and became a book club favorite across the country. But people just didn't connect with any of her follow-ups. I saw the impact that it had on her. She became constantly stressed, and the Mom I used to know pretty much disappeared. A part of me thinks she'll always be chasing that high of her first book, even if she will never get that back. It's gone.

"Speaking of, I've got to go, Sammy," says Mom. "Have a great night, okay?"

"You too."

I hang up and look around my room.

So this is it. College. I've gone to all this effort to change my life, and yet here I am, in my room by myself, planning on going to bed before seven. If I wanted to do this, I may as well have stayed at home. And also: Screw Mom for telling me what to do. She doesn't know me anymore, and she doesn't know what I am capable of.

I go through my phone and find the Alpha Phi Nu Rush Week page. The event tonight starts at six thirty, so I haven't missed it. It'll be close, but I think I can still make it. I already know what I'm going to do for the rest of the night if I stay here, and that's tie myself in knots over Mom. Sure, maybe joining a frat is diving into the deep end of having a social life, but it's better than the alternative. Plus, Dad told me I should go, and I trust his judgment a hell of a lot more than I trust Mom's. I read more about the event and see that there's a dress code: shirt and slacks. I need to dress to impress, apparently.

I grab my nicest shirt from my closet.

AΦN house is a sight to behold.

It's bigger than I was expecting, a mansion, really. Situated on Greek Row, it's a standout among a long stretch of fraternity and sorority houses, and from the looks of things, AΦN house is the biggest and nicest. It's brick, with eight white columns out front and AΦN in black on the facade of the house. It's at least two stories tall and has a large, well-kept yard. I'm not exactly sure what I was expecting—maybe for it to be a loud, messy house—but this place actually looks really nice.

I've just sprinted across campus to make it here, and I'm only a few minutes late. It doesn't help that I'm wearing slacks, a nice white shirt, and dress shoes that aren't exactly made for running. Add that to the unnatural heat, and I'm sure I look like a total mess by now. Good thing my hair is so short, but my face is sweaty and there are wet circles under my arms. I'll just have to stand with my arms pinned to my side so that people don't see.

A small group of well-dressed guys are standing on the steps of the house. I wipe my forehead on my sleeve, trying to mop up as much sweat as I can, then go up to one of the guys. He sticks his hand out.

"Hey, bro," he says. He speaks with a California drawl, matching his even tan. His outfit screams wealth but still seems kind of tacky: His just slightly pink shirt is tucked into white pants held up by a black belt, clashing with his gold watch and brown loafers. Still, he's cute. "I'm Brian, our treasurer."

"Sam."

"Good handshake there, Sam. Head on in."

I stop. My only real knowledge of fraternities has been from movies, and pretty much every fraternity movie I have seen has involved hazing of some sort. Oren didn't give me the impression that he was the kind of guy who thought it would be fun to bully a group of guys drawn in by the promise of a group of friends, but I did only meet him once. I just want to make sure I'm not going to walk in there and find a bunch of guys in hooded cloaks who tell me to do something weird like eat a goldfish to gain acceptance.

"What exactly is this?" I ask. "Oren invited me, but I don't really know what I'm getting myself into."

"It's rush, bro."

"Yeah, but what's that?"

"Well, this week you get to know us, and we get to know

you." He links his fingers. "If we match up, you become a pledge."

"And if not?"

"You go on your merry way. Don't stress, man, it's not a good look. I'll see you in there."

I go up the steps and take one last moment to look up before I go inside, passing through two heavy wooden doors. Inside is a hallway, the walls lined with dark wood. Hanging on the walls are framed group photos of past generations of brothers. Up against the wall is a stone bust of an old man. Even though it's spotless, there's a faint smell that's distinctly masculine in a way that isn't bad but is very noticeable. It smells like a bunch of different colognes mixing. I reach a glass case filled with trophies. I peer closer and see that these are all academic awards handed to the chapter. I hear sounds farther on, so I make my way down the hall, until I reach an open doorway that leads to a large living room.

Leather couches are dotted around the space, and there's an ancient pool table in the corner. Standing around the room is a bunch of guys, about half of whom have name tags stuck to their chests, all making small talk. Some of them turn their heads to glance at me, but then they return to their conversations.

By the pool table, I see Oren. He raises a hand and waves at me. There's a small table on the side, with the name stickers and a bunch of Sharpies. I write my name on one, then stick it on my chest before walking up to Oren. He's standing with three other guys. One is about as stereotypical a frat boy as I can imagine: He has bullish features and dark, deep-set eyes, as well as an intimidatingly bulky frame. Clearly he's proud of it, as his shirt is a size too small so it clings to every curve. His name tag reads TRIPP. The second, Mikey, is blond, and he has big, expressive blue eyes. He's dressed impeccably in a pink polo shirt that fits him so well it has to be tailored. The third is called Justin, and wait . . . I recognize him.

Justin. He's the streaker. While the other three are attractive, Justin is in a way that's sort of otherworldly. His features are perfectly symmetrical, and he has the poise of someone who knows just how to pose. Of them all, though, Oren is definitely the most my type.

"You made it," says Oren, seeming actually, genuinely pleased that I'm here.

I'm still tripping over the fact that I am looking at the streaker, as if he's a celebrity and I'm starstruck.

"Sam, meet the guys. This is our president, Tripp, and Mikey, our vice president, and Justin. Guys, meet Sam."

"Hey, man," says Mikey.

"Sup."

Justin waves.

"What makes you want to be an Alpha?" asks Tripp, then he takes a sip of his beer.

Oren and Mikey are both watching me. It dawns on me what this is, and I only just figure out that I should be nervous. I'm trying to impress them. All the other visitors here are my competition, and we're fighting for limited spots in the brotherhood. I'm rusty, but I used to pride myself on my ability to win people over, so I just need to do that. In the past, I've found that the best way to get people to like you is to be honest. Most people can sense a lie a mile away.

"I want to meet new people," I say. "I don't have too many friends right now, and I want to change that."

"You came to the right place," says Oren.

"And what would you offer the brotherhood in return?" asks Tripp. "What's special about you?"

"Um, good question." I think. "I'm a hard worker, I always give everything one hundred percent."

"That could describe almost anyone here," says Mikey as he crosses his arms. Tripp glances away from me and starts scanning the room. Crap. I'm losing them. "What's special about *you*?"

I think of telling them about my past. My first instinct is that I can't, but why can't I?

A part of me wants to keep who I really am a secret, but in reality, I know that won't last long. All it would take is one Google search in order for them to find out who I am. I can't hide it, unless I want to go to the extreme of faking my name, but that would mean I'm lying, and I'm not a fan of that. They're probably going to find out sooner or later. I may as well get some credit for it.

"Grab your phones," I say.

The brothers all take out their phones. Oren has the brand-new iPhone, the one that came out only a few days ago. I get a vibe that he's from serious money. I heard once somewhere that the way to tell if someone is truly wealthy is to check their shoes and watches, because loads of people buy flashy labels to try to look wealthy, but those items are harder to fake. Oren is wearing a smartwatch, and his shoes are stunning, clearly very expensive.

"My name's Sam Carville," I say.

They search for me.

"No fucking way," says Justin. "This is you?"

He's brought up an old picture of me. I get why Justin feels the need to ask this, as I look completely different. They used a photo of me from a day I went to the beach with Eli just after my sixteenth birthday, so a few months before Lake Priest. I'm sitting in the sun, and Eli had just cracked a joke, so I'm captured mid-laugh. I only vaguely look like that guy anymore.

"Yep."

"Fuck, man," says Mikey. "Way to bury the lede."

"Pledging can be tough," says Tripp. "You sure you're ready for it?"

He isn't joking, but this notion is funny to me.

"After what I've been through," I say, "I think I can handle whatever a group of frat boys throws at me. No offense."

"None taken," says Oren.

Tripp and Justin seem surprised and impressed by my bluntness, but Mikey starts to scowl. Oh well. Three out of four isn't bad.

"But seriously," I say. "I think maybe being a brother might be a good thing for me."

Oren's head tilts to the side. "Why?"

"I've kind of stopped living for the past two years. I want to start again. It'll be hard, but I'm up for it because I don't want the worst thing that ever happened to me to define me forever."

"Good answer," says Oren.

Mikey rolls his eyes. Okay, I'm not sure what that's about, but there's some tension between the two.

"Wait here," says Tripp, and he walks away. I watch him cross the room, grab a can of beer, and come back. He cracks it open and hands it to me. I take it. I haven't been much of a drinker. I've only had a few sips before, but I'm eighteen now. I can handle a beer.

I take a sip, and it's actually pretty nice. It's not like soda or anything, but it's good, kind of sour. Tripp claps me lightly on the shoulder, and a warm feeling spreads through my chest. He gave me a beer. For such a classic frat guy as Tripp, this feels like the ultimate mark of respect. He knows my story, and his reaction was to get me a beer. For so long I've been worried that people would judge me harshly, or want to avoid me, but maybe that fear was unfounded.

"So," says Justin. "Do you play any sports?"

"I used to play lacrosse but haven't in a while."

"Oh hey, same," says Oren.

"Why'd you quit?" asks Mikey.

"Um, I wasn't really in a place to give it my all, I guess. Do you guys play anything?"

"Basketball," says Mikey.

"I surf," says Justin.

"Football," says Tripp.

"Who said something about football?" says a guy named Drew, and he joins in the conversation. Drew's got jet-black hair styled up into a perfect wave and high cheek-bones. He is total dreamboat material. His outfit is simple but perfect, with each item fitting exactly right, and he's accessorized with a stunning watch and really nice shoes.

It all feels totally normal. They know about me, and they're curious, sure, but nobody is treating me any different. As Tripp starts telling a story about his victory last year against the Hollifield Ravens, complete with a recording on his phone of his triumphant touchdown, Oren sidles up to me.

"Having fun?" asks Oren, his voice low.

"I am, yeah."

"Good, 'cause I want you to know we're here for you, if you need extra help."

"Yeah, definitely."

"Good. Because bravery is what we look for, and you're definitely brave."

He glances up and down, checking me out.

I feel butterflies.

Chapter Six

RUSH WEEK CALENDAR

Monday: Meet the Pikes 6:30 p.m. at House

Tuesday: Pool Night with Zeta Chi 7 p.m. Meet at House

Wednesday: Patriots Game 6 p.m. Meet at House

Thursday: Pickup BBall 5 p.m. at MU Gym

Friday: Pizza 'n' Poker 6 p.m. at House

Saturday: Pig Roast 6 p.m. at House

Sunday: Pinning 5 p.m. at Conference Room 3A, Webster Building

I check the calendar on my phone again and am glad that I have a week until classes start, because rush week is turning out to be a pretty massive commitment. I'm not complaining—it all sounds fun, but it's just a *lot*. Like, if I go to everything, this will be more social activities in one week than I've been to all year. Maybe the weirdest thing is that I'm not worried about it, it all seems fun.

The alarm on my phone goes off, which means it's time to go.

I check my reflection in the mirror one last time and then leave my room to head to the house.

I'm exactly on time.

Some rushes are already waiting around the entrance of the house, dressed in trunks and T-shirts or tank tops. The sun has already set, so the campus is lit by iron streetlights. I go up to the group.

"Hey, man," says the one closest to me, a thin guy with short copper-colored hair and square glasses perched on his nose. He's probably twenty pounds lighter than most of the guys here, and he has an incredibly friendly face. His T-shirt has Florence Pugh from *Midsommar* on it. Great. A horror fan. Horror movies are one of my past interests that vanished after what happened. I tried watching a slasher movie once and got about five minutes into the movie before I had to turn it off because I was feeling so unwell.

"I'm Josh," says the guy.

"Sam," I say.

His eyes widen a fraction. "Wait, you're Sam Carville, right? People have been saying you're on campus."

"You're famous?" asks Drew.

Another guy hears this and joins in. "Who's famous?"

This guy is good-looking in a carefree, scruffy way, with handsome features almost hidden by his patchy beard and unkept brown curls. He has pretty eyes, an unusual light green color. I can smell the distinct, earthy smell of weed on him.

"I'm Booker, by the way," he says, offering his hand.

"Sam, and I'm not famous," I say as we shake. "Something happened to me two years ago, something people know about.

"Have you heard of the Lake Priest murders?"

"Dude," says Drew. "You were there?"

"Fuck," says Booker. "I thought that was an urban legend."

"Unfortunately not."

"Shit, man," says Booker. "Well, I'm glad you survived."

"Me too," I say.

Down the street, a large van turns the corner, drives up to us, and parks.

The passenger-side door slides open. Tripp is inside, in what I feel is his typical outfit: a loud tank top with FRAT DADDY across the chest and loose shorts. His eyes are covered by neon sunglasses, the handles tucked into his dark brown curls.

"All right, boys!" he calls from the front passenger seat. "Pile in!"

We climb into the van, and I find myself squashed in between Josh and Booker in the back seat, with Drew a row in front of us. I don't want to judge or anything, but the smell of weed coming from Booker is a lot. The car fills with prospective pledges, leaving another few groups to get in a different van. I'd say maybe forty people are coming tonight, and I wonder what that means for my odds. If forty people apply, how many get in?

In the driver's seat is Mikey, who is watching me, his clear blue eyes cautious in the rearview. His attention darts away. A few other potential pledges climb in, and then Tripp slams the door closed. Mikey is good-looking, so I don't mind him looking at me. I just wish he had a little more kindness in his eyes.

Mikey starts the engine, and the van pulls onto the road.

"All right, boys," says Tripp, turning around in his seat to face us. "You aren't brothers yet, so be on your best behavior, all right?"

"Yes, sir!" calls Booker.

"That's the spirit."

Tripp turns the music up, making a Travis Scott song play even louder.

"Hell yes," says Booker. "I love this song."

In front of us, Drew's face falls.

"What's wrong?" asks Booker.

"Nothing," says Drew.

It's a clear lie, something is assuredly up. Drew seems uncomfortable. Of all the guys here, he reminds me of my past self the most. Drew's a little preppy, clearly cares about his presentation. Unlike me, he seems like he was one of the most popular boys at the school he went to before this. He just has that air that he was universally beloved once. It must be hard for him to come here, too, and start over. I'm sure everyone will soon love Drew as well.

"So," says Josh. "What's your major?"

My eyes fall to his shirt. He must really love horror to want to display it on his clothes. Or maybe he's just trying to show what makes him distinct, hoping he will get the attention of the brothers. That makes sense. Even though this seems like it's just for fun, it's not. This event, and all events like it, are for the brothers to evaluate us in order to decide if they want us in the brotherhood.

"Psychology," I say.

"Why psychology?"

Even over the music, I can tell Drew and Booker are listening.

"My therapist helped me a lot," I say. "After. I'd like to do that for someone else."

"That's awesome," says Josh.

"Truly," says Booker. "Using something bad to do good is, like, incredible."

"I'm intimidated now," says Drew.

"Why?" I ask.

"There's no way you're not getting in."

"He's right," says Booker. "You'd have to do something really stupid to mess this up."

"Thanks. How about you guys—what are your majors?"

"Film," says Josh. "Shocker, I know."

"Exercise science," says Drew.

"I haven't picked yet," says Booker. "Maybe teaching. I want to try some stuff out, see what clicks."

"Catch!"

Something is tossed my way, and I catch it. It's a pair of sunglasses wrapped in clear plastic, with the handles in bright neon. Each of the rushes has been tossed a pair, all in different colors. Mine are aqua, and printed along the sides is I ♡ GREEK LIFE. Each of the other prospective pledges are tossed their own glasses.

Josh opens his, which are lime green, and he puts them on. Drew's are the same shade as mine, and Booker's are orange.

"Isn't it douchey to wear sunglasses at night?" I ask.

"I think you just have to lean into it," says Josh.

I open my sunglasses and put them on. Now everyone is wearing them, and I've got to say, it's kind of cool. I got lucky, too, because blue is my favorite color. I usually like a deeper blue, like the color of the ocean as opposed to this radioactive shade, but it's close enough.

"I have to confess something," says Josh. "I've read your mom's book."

Oh.

It's not the most shocking thing, because a lot of people have. If we were on good terms, I'd be over the moon that her audience includes wannabe frat boys, but we're not, so I'm a little upset. Now Josh will have a preconceived idea of who I am.

"What'd you think?" I ask.

"I liked it! I know it's marketed as a thriller, but it's totally a horror. If you have someone in a mask, then it's automatically horror."

I just bob my head.

"I heard they're making a movie," says Josh, clearly missing that I'd prefer to talk about anything else, even if I am trying to show that with my expression. Maybe he's missing it because of these damn sunglasses. "Is that still happening?"

"I dunno, Mom and I don't really talk much."

Josh winces. "Fair, sorry I brought it up."

About ten minutes later, we reach our destination and all climb out. It's a pool in front of a hotel, and pumping music is playing loudly. A DJ is set up in a cabana at the back of the pool, and the whole place is lit only by the moonlight and strings of golden lights that have been wrapped around the palm trees.

About fifty guys, and maybe the same number of girls, are already standing around the pool or swimming. There are tents set up along the edges of the pool, where even more are hanging out.

Led by Tripp and Mikey, we all go to a tented area, where a few of the other brothers are sitting. I see Oren resting on a giant blow-up swan, his shirt unbuttoned. He also has a pair of cheap yellow sunglasses on. Most of the other pledges have their eyes on the sorority girls, who are standing in groups and are showing a lot of skin, but I kind of can't take my eyes off Oren. He's freaking dazzling.

A voice tells me that I can't go there, because boys are off-limits, and I should try to turn off my obvious attraction to him. But why not? I'm not with Eli anymore, and we ended on good terms. And yet, I still feel guilty for even noticing. I think it's because for the entire time I was dating Eli, I was sure that he was the guy for me. I remember thinking just how perfect it was, and how I was going to be with him forever. And now I'm here, and I have no idea where he is.

"Sam?"

Wait, I recognize that voice. I turn and see Alyson Flores, a girl I was friends with in high school, staring at me. She's cut her brown hair short, but other than that she looks pretty much the same as I remember her, dressed in a cute outfit I'm sure is in fashion right now. We actually used to be close, until I retreated from the world. I remember her really trying to reach out to me after the lake, but I always ignored her messages, because I ignored basically everyone who reached out. From memory, she tried harder than most.

"Hey," I say.

She drags her bottom lip across her teeth, and there's obvious hurt in her eyes. I get it; I did ghost her.

And now she's here, looking at me like I drowned a bunch of puppies in front of her. Which is fair.

We move a small way away from the group and find a quiet spot around the tent. Farther down, there's a dark area. I watch it for a moment. It would be a perfect place for a killer to hide. I wish I could be happy to see her, because she's an amazing person: smart, funny, and creative. She wanted to be a singer, and I remember she had a major role in the school musical, a part that normally would go to a senior. She got it because she was that good.

"Do you go to Munroe?" she asks. Her arms are crossed, and her nails are digging into her forearm.

"Yeah."

"And you're joining a frat?"

"Yep."

"You could've told me," she says.

"I—I know. I'm sorry."

"Are you even happy to see me?"

"I am, I just . . ."

Hurt twists her features. *Just* is her answer. I know that it sucks, and it's unfair of me, but the truth is that even if I do miss her friendship, I'm not the happiest to see her here. She is like a giant flashing reminder of my past, the one I want so badly to move on from. I glance again at the dark spot, making sure nobody is lurking there.

"Fine," she says. She turns and walks away, crossing the party to go to who I am guessing are her new sorority friends. I go back over to my group, joining a conversation with Oren.

"Who was that?" he asks.

"We used to be friends," I say.

"Used to be?"

"I kinda ghosted her after the lake."

"Oof."

"Tell me about it. I feel bad."

Oren shakes his head. "Don't. You did the best you could. If she doesn't get that, she's not a good friend." He glances down. "Do you want a beer?"

"So badly."

Oren turns to Josh, beside me. "How about you, Stargensky?"

"No thanks, I don't drink."

"Lee? Wilkins?"

Both Drew and Booker accept Oren's offer.

"Coming right up," says Oren. He claps me on the shoulder, leaving his hand there for a moment. "Make yourselves comfortable."

Booker sits down on the inflatable swan and puts his arms behind his head. He's taken off his shirt, showing a pale and surprisingly furry chest. "This is the life."

Oren walks away to get our beers.

"What's going on there?" asks Drew.

"Huh?"

"I picked up a vibe between you and Oren. Are you two . . ."

"What? No," I say.

"Ah. But you want to be. Because you are gay, right?"

"How'd you tell?"

"You were just checking out Booker. I have weirdly good gaydar for a straight guy. I'd say I have about a ninety-five percent success rate."

"I don't," says Josh. "I had no idea my brother was gay until he told me. My mind was *blown*. Looking back, it was pretty obvious. Like he kept having guys over, and they'd spend all their time hanging out in his room with the door locked."

"Does he go here?" I ask.

Josh shakes his head. "He went to New York the second

he could. He wants to be a playwright, and he says there isn't much of a playwright scene here. Drew, I have a challenge for you."

"Shoot."

"Who else is gay here? If your gaydar is as good as you say it is, it should be easy."

Drew scans the crowd, searching. Tripp is currently in the process of drinking a can of beer as fast as he can. I know gay guys come in all sorts, but he seems very straight.

Drew spots Mikey. He too has pulled off his shirt and is currently taking some selfies, making sure to get in his abs. "Oh, Mikey's gay; that's easy."

"Why is that easy?"

It wasn't obvious to me, I didn't really get a queer vibe from him at all. With his military-style hair, I thought he might be an army brat.

"He and Oren dated last year," says Josh.

"How do you know that?"

"My sister is in Sigma Phi. It's all anyone talked about last year. They got together and it was this huge thing, and then they broke up and it was an even bigger deal."

Oren returns, and we all clam up.

"Ah," he says. "Were you talking about the breakup?"

"No," says Booker. "We were talking about . . . fine, we were."

"It's old news," says Oren. "We're friends now, it's fine. I'm thinking of going for a walk. Sam, want to join me?"

"Yeah, okay."

We set off. Now it's just me and Oren's very distracting smile. I feel a prickle on the back of my neck, so I turn, and Mikey is death-staring me.

"What's wrong?" asks Oren.

"Mikey was just death-staring me."

"He tends to do that."

We walk around the pool in silence. Candy-colored lights illuminate the place. Back at the tent, Tripp lets out a wild yell, then runs and jumps into the pool. A few brothers join him. Oren and I find a quiet pair of chairs and sit down. I glance around. We're away from the main group, but not so far that I couldn't get back to the crowd quickly if I needed to. If someone did want to attack me, here would be a pretty bad place to do it, because there wouldn't be anywhere they could go to escape. That's a little comforting, but as I am anywhere unfamiliar, I'm on edge.

I'm doing well, though. I still have my nerves, I never expect them to go away completely. They aren't ruining my enjoyment of the night, though.

"Do you have any exes?" asks Oren.

"Yeah, one."

"Do you talk anymore?"

"Nope."

"That's fair. Mikey and I have tried to be friends, but I don't know if it's working."

I adjust in my seat. "When'd you break up?"

"About six months ago. Sometimes it still feels like yesterday, though."

"I'm sorry."

"You didn't do anything. But I sometimes wonder, like . . ."

"What?"

"Well, when I meet someone new, I'm worried about how he'll react."

A part of me hopes *I* could be that someone new. Which is surprising. Before I got here, I didn't think I would have any interest in dating or even hooking up. I'm still not sure I do, but it's undeniable that Oren is cute. *Incredibly* cute. He could be a movie star with looks like this. It's clear who he'd play: He'd be the sweet, perfect boy next door.

"But anyway, I'm sick of talking about Mikey. Want to go in?"

"It is why we're here, right?"

He blinks, then smiles, showing off his straight teeth. "You're messing with me?"

"I am."

"I like you, Carville."

Oren takes off his shirt, and I kick off my shoes and do the same. I know it's not polite to stare, but that's what I want to do right now, because Oren is so handsome. His chest is lean, but with defined muscles. He doesn't seem to be the type to spend hours in a gym or chug protein shakes, but he's clearly athletic. We make our way over to the edge of the water, and Oren steps in. It's a lagoon pool, starting shallow and slowly getting deeper, so it only reaches his mid calves.

"It's cold," he says, and he hugs his arms to his lithe body.

I step in after him. His eyes move down to my chest. I wish he was checking me out, but he's looking at my scar.

"You can ask about it," I say. "It's really ugly, I know."

"It's not ugly," he says. "Not even a little."

I smile. I'd forgotten what it feels like, and this emotion is better than anything, the most thrilling thing on earth. His dark brown eyes meet mine.

"You're single, right?" he asks.

"Maybe. Why?"

This feels like a dream. A hot frat guy is flirting with me. I know my flirting skills are bad; it's never been something I've been good at. I haven't really cared about that for a long time, though. Now, I feel like I want to practice, because this is fun.

Oren grins. "Just checking."

Chapter Seven

I freeze, rooted to the spot. I've just left my dorm room, and Oren's in the hallway, with only a towel wrapped around his waist. His hair is still slightly wet, and he smells of body-wash. My mind goes completely blank. It's way too early in the day to be presented with such a life-changing sight.

"Morning, Carville," he says. "How's your head?"

"Sore."

It's the truth. I didn't even think to answer with one of *Drag Race*'s famous responses to that question. I wound up having a few beers at the pool party last night, enough to get a buzz going. It was great, and I totally relaxed, but I'm paying for that now, as my temples are throbbing.

Oren smiles, and it's dazzling. "I do know an amazing hangover cure, if you're free."

"Yeah, sure. Just want to take a shower first."

"Avoid the third one, it's bad. Meet back here in five minutes?"

He slides past me, and I don't think I was prepared to be this close to a fit, shirtless frat boy. That's something I need to prepare for, for sure. I go to the bathroom. One of the showers is being used, and a guy is brushing his teeth by a sink. I brave the third stall, picking the one closest to the door, strip, and get into the shower. I turn on the tap, and a steady spray of water comes out.

When I close my eyes, what I find myself thinking about is Oren.

Oren's hangover cure turns out to be a Bloody Mary and a grilled cheese. He made it on a press he has above his mini fridge.

"Bottoms up," he says as he hands me the drink he just finished making.

His room is actually amazing: He has a loft bed, and under it is a fairly large couch facing a huge TV. He has all the latest gaming consoles, as well as a stack of games I would love to play. An *Avengers* poster is on the wall beside a bunch of notebooks.

I try the drink and pull a face. It's freaking disgusting. I don't like tomato, celery, or the unmissable sting of alcohol, so this is a nightmare.

"It works, trust me," he says.

I've already eaten the grilled cheese, which was great. Having more alcohol right now feels like a mistake.

"Wait, is this your first hangover?" he asks.

"I'm not a saint. But it's my first in a while."

"Aww, buddy. How do you feel?"

"Like death."

I force down another mouthful of Bloody Mary. As I drink, I notice a row of journalism text books. Crap. Oren might be pretty incredible in every other way, but I'm not sure I can trust someone who's studying journalism. Not after the way the press treated me after the lake. I suffered, and they saw dollar signs.

"Do you want a coffee?" he asks. "I'd offer to make you one, but I'm the worst at it. Plus the cafeteria coffee is actually pretty good."

"I'll have to see that for myself."

"Just wait for your mind to be blown."

We walk down the hallway, and I am all too aware how close he is to me. Not because he's a threat or anything, just because he's a boy, and him standing close is a big deal. He's put on some manly cologne, and it smells incredible: like cedar and cloves.

We swipe our meal plan cards at the turnstile in our dorm's dining hall.

My phone buzzes.

How are you doing?

"Who's that?" asks Oren.

"Dad, checking in."

I text him back that I'm fine.

"That's nice of him."

"Yeah, he's the best."

"So you're close?"

"Yeah, very close. Are you close with yours?"

"God no. My dad's a lawyer; he has more important things to do than spend time with me."

His face falls.

"I'm sorry," I say.

"Shocking, right? I'm a gay dude with daddy issues."

He picks at his rainbow bracelet.

"Do you always wear that?" I ask.

"Just during rush."

"Why?"

"I guess I want potential pledges to know they're welcome, no matter how they identify."

"That's really nice of you."

"I'm glad you think so."

He smiles at me, and those damn butterflies come back.

"Have you picked a major?"

"Psych. You're doing journalism, right?"

"Yeah."

"Why'd you pick that?"

"Good question. It always seemed really noble to me."

I have to stop myself from raising an eyebrow. "Noble?"

He reads my expression, and he leans back a little.

"There are bad journalists out there, sure. But I want to be one of the good ones. I don't want to write stories about celebrities or tragedies. I want to expose the rich and the powerful, and make sure everyone knows the things they want to keep behind closed doors."

After my experiences with them, I never thought I could appreciate journalism. But now I see it.

"Are you coming to dinner tonight?" he asks.

"Are you?"

"Yep."

"Then yeah."

He smiles again. "Sweet."

I'm not sure exactly where things are going with Oren. He's cute, sure. Like, really cute. And I am most definitely attracted to him. Those things can exist without me wanting to date him, though. If I'm honest with myself, the thought of dating someone other than Eli still feels a little strange. When I look forward into the future, I don't see myself being single forever. And yet, I haven't had a moment where I have had the surefire thought that I am ready to date.

There is always hooking up, but that feels wrong with Oren, too. I think if I could pick anything, I would choose to date him.

This is very new, and the most surprising thing is that it doesn't scare me at all.

"Okay, boys," says Tripp. "The rules are simple."

It's Thursday and I've joined the rushes and some of the brothers on the basketball court. We're standing in a line, listening to Tripp. So far, I've been to every rush event, and I've always had a great time. This one worries me, though, because I haven't played a sport in a while . . . and Oren is in the bleachers, watching.

"A three-pointer decides possession, and we play in four v four. Pick your teams."

I go with Josh (who is wearing a gym outfit that I'm pretty sure he's never worn before, as I can see the tag hanging out the back of his shirt), Drew, and Booker.

"Here," I say, and I pull the tag off Josh's shirt.

"Thanks," he says.

"No problem."

"You four," says Tripp. "On the court."

He blows his whistle. We're going up against a team of brothers, including Justin and Mikey. Oh great. I'm up against Oren's ex. That's exactly what I want.

"We shoot for possession," says Justin, and he bounces the ball to Drew.

Drew bounces the ball to the three-point line, then shoots. It sails right in.

I give Drew a high five.

The game begins.

It becomes pretty obvious that Mikey is the only one

who can actually play. He's so fast that he can easily get around us. I don't really care, though, because this is fun. The brothers are a much better team, almost totally in sync. They pass the ball around me, then Justin shoots and scores.

All right. Game on.

Drew passes me the ball, and I bounce it forward. I pass it to Josh and run around Justin. I'm open. Josh tosses the ball to me, and I get into position in order to shoot, and I throw it.

Mikey jumps up and swats the ball down hard.

"Nice try," he says, grinning.

Soon the timer runs out, and we lose by thirty points. It could've been worse, especially because we were up against Mikey.

"Good game," says Justin, and he shakes my hand. He smiles, and it's stunning. I shake the hand of the next brother, until I make it to Mikey.

He goes past me without a single word or acknowledgment. It's like I'm not even there. He just brushes by. Anger builds within me. The past me would just take this hit, but screw that. I've been through way too much to let anyone openly disrespect me.

"Dude," I say.

He spins around. "What?"

"You didn't shake my hand."

"Sorry, princess." He offers his hand.

I shake it. He squeezes my hand too hard. I walk off the court, and the next group of rushes takes our place. I go up to Oren and sit down, still fuming. He and Oren aren't together anymore—Mikey can't act like this. It's so immature.

"I saw," says Oren. "I'm sorry."

"It's fine."

Oren looks away, clearly wanting to move on. On the court, a new game starts. Booker gets the ball and shoots, but misses.

"You're really good," says Oren.

"Thanks."

"Like that three-pointer you got? Amazing. Have you ever thought of playing?"

"No, but that was fun."

Oren clears his throat and slides an inch closer to me.

I don't move away.

Chapter Eight

"Oren?"

We're standing in front of Lake Priest, staring out at the huge stretch of still, dark water.

Oren is on the rocky shoreline, his hands tucked into his pockets, waiting for me. Behind him is a forest of towering Douglas firs, covered in a pale fog. It's twilight, and I can just identify the outline of the nearly full moon in the sky. Oren looks as handsome as always, a classic, all-American frat boy, even down to his dark-blue-and-red varsity jacket. He shouldn't be here. Nothing good happens to boys like him at Lake Priest.

"You made it," he says, pulling his hands out.

"What are you doing here?" I ask.

"Very funny. You texted me."

The sun is setting rapidly now, too fast, and it's already getting dark. Crickets are chirping, and there's an unnatural silence around the whole place. Night is *his* time, and that means we can't be here.

"Let's go," I say.

I grab his wrist and try to pull him forward. I don't have time to explain, not right now. I can later.

He shakes me off. "Sam, stop. You're freaking me out. What's going on?"

"Someone's after us. We need to go."

A branch snaps.

"What was that?" Oren asks. He clenches his jaw tight and swallows.

I can't bring myself to say it. It's *him*. He's here, because of course he is.

I break into a sprint, and Oren follows after me. We run down the path that leads back to the house. I run as fast as I can, a full sprint. Trees whip past me in a blur. I can't keep this up for long, but I know I don't have a choice. Oren is easily keeping pace. Behind me, I can hear footsteps and heavy, labored breathing. I don't need to look to know that it's him.

We run around a corner and see the house. Only it's too late. It's a burned, blackened husk of what it should be. There's nothing left but charred walls and ash. Max's car is parked in the lot. I go up to it and try the door. It's locked. Fuck.

We're trapped.

I turn around.

Shawn is standing in the middle of the road, holding his knife. He moves quickly, rushing toward Oren. Oren raises his hands, but he's too slow. The knife sinks into his stomach as he's pushed up against the car. He gasps as the blade is pulled out, then is plunged back in again. A scream is trapped in my throat. Oren staggers forward, then falls to his knees. Blood seeps into the material of his shirt.

Oren looks up at me, begging for an explanation. He doesn't understand. He doesn't know he's going to die.

"Why did you bring me here?" he asks.

"I . . . I don't know."

He's probably never come close to death before, so he doesn't know what it's like. How unfair it feels, and how it makes everything that's happened in your life feel so small, because it hasn't been enough, and suddenly it's over.

Shawn moves behind Oren and positions the blade in front of his throat. He grips Oren's hair and pulls his head up, exposing his neck. Before I can say anything, the knife slices across, drawing a line of blood. He pushes Oren, who falls forward and lands facedown. Oren shudders as more blood gushes out, and his eyes glaze over.

I sit up, gasping for air.

I'm in my dorm room, and it's still and quiet, and the only noise is the soft whir of the fan. I'm safe. It was just a nightmare. A horrible, incredibly grim nightmare, but that's all it was. Still, the feelings of it remain, as if I really was just there, as if I really did watch Oren get killed by my worst enemy.

I'm okay.

I groan and lie back down, resting my head against my damp pillow. My body is covered in a layer of sweat, and my heart is still racing dangerously fast. I must've been bucking and kicking in my sleep, as I've kicked off my covers, so they're bunched up around my legs.

I glance across the room, and there is an envelope resting in the middle of the floor, clearly slid under the door while I was sleeping. It's bid day tomorrow. Actually, it's past midnight, which would mean today is bid day.

Holy shit.

I'm about to find out whether I made it into Alpha Phi Nu.

I scoop up the envelope, then rip it open.

We, the brothers of Alpha Phi Nu,
have chosen to cordially invite

Sam Carville

To join our brotherhood

Behind my bid is another letter, inviting me to a pinning ceremony this afternoon in a conference room near the quad, along with another piece of folded paper, with a note written in neat handwriting.

> Congrats! I'm not supposed to tell you this, but it was nearly unanimous. See you at the ceremony.
>
> —Oren ☺

Nearly unanimous?

DID YOU GET IN????

It's a text from Josh that I just received. Soft sunlight is coming in through my window, and I feel well-rested. I smile.

I did! Did you?

YESSS! I knew you would. I did as well. Drew and Booker both did, too. We're going to be brothers!!!

So what if someone, presumably Mikey, opposed me? Almost everyone else was in support. And I'm not going to give up on something I'm actually starting to really enjoy because what, Mikey doesn't like that his ex has been flirting with me? Oren's a free agent, and it's been six months since they broke up. They aren't together, but Oren isn't allowed to be with anyone else? How is that fair?

I go to Instagram and scroll through Oren's followers until I find Mikey. He doesn't post much, but it's clear his family is wealthy, as there are pictures of him on expensive boats, and on vacations in places like Morocco and Japan. His family lives in a large mansion, and Mikey has posted a few times lounging by the pool. No matter how nice the mood appears to be, he never seems to smile in any of the pictures. I scroll down, searching for Oren, but if there were any pictures of them together, they have been deleted.

What happened there? Did they just grow apart, or did something cause them to break up?

And why am I even looking up Mikey's Instagram?

I get a new text from Josh.

Do you want to get breakfast at Southside? Drew, Booker, and I are going to celebrate.

Sounds great!

By the time I make it to Southside, Josh, Drew, and Booker are already there, waiting by the entrance.

"Congrats," I say.

"Thanks, congrats to you, too!" says Josh. "I got really nervous that I wasn't going to get a bid. I slept so badly last night."

"Same," says Drew.

"You all need to smoke more," says Booker. "I slept fine."

We swipe our meal plan cards and go inside. We go up to the omelet station and join the small line.

"What happens now?" I ask Drew.

"We accept the bids at the ceremony tonight, and then we'll be pledges for the rest of the term."

"And what does that mean?"

We shuffle forward.

"They'll test us and see if they actually want us in the brotherhood," says Booker. "It'll be fun, though. There should be heaps of parties and plenty of hookup opportunities."

We get our omelets and go back to our table. It seems like a little group is forming with us four, and I honestly couldn't be more thrilled. Each of them seems great.

"Can I get your advice?" says Drew to the group. We all nod. "I'm long distance with my girlfriend, right? And it's great, but . . ."

"What?"

"Well, we're going to be pledges tonight. And that means there's going to be a lot of girls around."

"I can stay near you if you want," says Josh. "I repel girls."

"With that attitude you will," says Booker.

"I'm serious," says Drew. "I love her. But there are so many girls here, and I'm worried I might want to do something."

"Have you talked to her?" I ask.

"She'd get so upset if she finds out I'm even thinking about this."

"But you *are* thinking about it," says Booker.

"Yeah," says Drew, sadly.

Booker scratches his arm. "Doesn't seem healthy to me, man."

"Then what should I do?" asks Drew.

"Talk to her," I say. The others agree.

"All right. I'll do it after this."

Drew lets out a puff of air, then digs into his omelet. I take a bite of mine. It's good; maybe not as good as one Dad would make, but it's still nice.

"Has anything happened with you and Oren?" asks Josh.

"What do you mean?"

"Everyone thinks you're going to hook up," says Booker, stating it like a fact.

"We might, but I dunno."

"Why wouldn't you?" asks Drew. "You're single, right?"

"Yeah, but I wasn't really planning on getting into anything serious."

"Who says it needs to be serious?" offers Booker. "This is college. It'd be a bad idea to tie yourself down. No offense, Drew."

"None taken."

Maybe they're right. The only thing stopping me is myself.

I'm getting sick of doing that.

Chapter Nine

"Welcome, everyone," says Tripp, "to this term's pinning ceremony."

Tripp has stuffed his large body into a suit, complete with a yellow bow tie. He's reading a prewritten speech off index cards. "My name is Neil Tripp, and I'm the president of Alpha Phi Nu. I'm excited to be performing this ceremony today. Alpha Phi Nu is an organization built on brotherhood and trust, and we welcome only exceptional men." He clears his throat. "Today I invite the outstanding men beside me to become pledges of our historic chapter."

We're in a conference room facing the rest of the brothers. Everyone is wearing suits or blazers. In the crowd, Oren notices me watching him, and he gives me a thumbs-up.

"It is our hope," continues Tripp, addressing the pledges, "that throughout your pledging process, you will develop a better understanding of the values of our fraternity and will develop the loyalty to the brotherhood that our historic organization deserves. We search for high quality, not a high quantity of men, as reflected by the small number we have invited here today. We recognize you as leaders of tomorrow, men who will shape the world and pride themselves on their integrity, loyalty, and bravery, the three touchstones of an Alpha Phi Nu brother."

I sit up straighter.

"Our fraternity has a history of civic and academic excellence, since our founding in 1894, and we believe each of you will continue to uphold the high standard of our forebears. Each of you has been assigned a big brother, who will be there for you as a friend and mentor. Now, repeat after me. I . . ."

We speak as a group. "I . . ."

"State your name."

Everyone does.

"Pledge to uphold the values of integrity, loyalty, and bravery, and to learn and honor all Alpha Phi Nu traditions."

We all say it back to him.

"I pledge to excel in my studies and to be an upstanding member of the Munroe University community."

A few people stumble on words near the end, but I manage to get them all right.

"I pledge my body, mind, and heart to Alpha Phi Nu."

I say it.

"Congratulations," says Tripp. "You're now officially pledges."

The crowd of brothers snap their fingers.

"Now, to demonstrate his support, your big brother will present you with your pledge pin and handbook. When I state your name, please stand. First is Drew Lee."

Drew stands up.

"Your big brother is Michael Datzman."

Mikey stands and does up the button of his blazer. I hate noticing it, but he's in the nicest outfit of everyone here. While some of the other clothes are ill-fitting or in colors that don't work together, Mikey looks ready to hit a red carpet in a sleek navy blazer, caramel chinos, patterned socks, and tan dress shoes. The whole look just works. He reaches Drew, hands him a hardcover book with the fraternity coat of arms on the front, and then pulls a pin from his pocket and sticks it to Drew's lapel. Once he's done, they both return to their seats.

"Samuel Carville."

I stand.

"Your big brother is Oren Fisher."

Oren gets up and approaches. Dizziness washes over me. Does this mean that he picked me? While his clothes might not look as expensive as Mikey's, he still looks incredible, and there's something totally charming in his choice of a bright green tie.

He hands me the book. Then he puts the pin on my lapel.

"Congrats," he whispers.

From this moment on, I'm not just Sam Carville, the guy who survived Lake Priest.

As of this second, I'm something else, too.

Chapter Ten

I hate him so much.

Justin leans against his kitchen counter and smiles at his phone. He's just gotten home from the gym, so he's a little sweaty, and he's still in his workout gear. He swipes through on his phone and calls the person who messaged him—Mikey. He and Mikey have been friends since they were both freshman, and Justin loves the guy, even if he does take basically everything way too seriously. Honestly, he broods so much that he would give Batman a run for his money. Mikey needs to calm down, that much is obvious.

As his phone rings, Justin starts making himself a protein shake, holding his phone to his ear with his shoulder. He's alone but doesn't have a care in the world. This is his house, after all. There's no way he'd be able to afford this place by himself, but thankfully his parents are both very generous. When he had to choose between living here or at the frat house with the rest of his brothers, the choice was obvious. He does love the guys, but Justin likes things to be clean, and the only time that house is clean is when the brothers make the pledges clean it before a party.

"Hello?" says Mikey.

"Sam bothering you again?"

Mikey sighs. "Yes."

"I dunno, I kinda like the guy."

Justin seals up his jumbo-sized bag of protein powder. He opens a cabinet, revealing rows and rows of sealed protein powders. He buys them in bulk online, because it's way cheaper that way, and he goes through so much of the stuff that he could face financial ruin if he bought it at full price. Justin shoves the one he just used into the cabinet and then closes the door.

"I do want to remind you that a few days ago you were worried we wouldn't get enough pledges," says Justin.

"I said I was worried we wouldn't get enough *good* pledges."

"Dude, you're jealous. I thought you were over Oren."

"I am."

"Then why all the Sam hate?"

"I told you, I get a bad vibe."

Justin goes through to the living room and turns on his PlayStation. Then he drops back onto his black leather couch and spreads his legs, getting comfortable. He has the place to himself for a few hours, which is something he thought he would enjoy more than he actually does.

He likes his housemate, Cody, even if he does have a few annoying habits, like having loud conversations in the living room while he's trying to sleep, or leaving his clothes in the washing machine for an entire day.

"Want to play some *MK?*" asks Justin.

"I can't, I've got to get ready for rush. So do you, unless you're planning on being fashionably late again."

"You know it. Come on, I'm bored."

"Ask Cody."

"He's not home yet, he's got some family thing. It's just me, all alone."

"You'll live. Gotta go, talk later."

"Love you," says Justin.

There's a pause.

"I love you, too."

Mikey hangs up, and Justin decides to take a few photos of himself, because he loves how he looks after a workout. He takes a few pictures, then uploads the best one to his Story. He doesn't even need a filter to make his teeth look perfectly white. Even though Justin knows it's slightly weird to be proud of your teeth, he is. He has a whole routine to keep them spotlessly white that he found from a video blogger, and he does that almost religiously. It works, too, and even some of the people in high positions in the modeling industry that he has met have complimented him on his teeth and have asked him where he went to get them done.

He lied and said it was a family secret. Models are supposed to be a little mysterious, after all. Modeling is never going to be his main thing, though: It pays well, but he doesn't want to be out of a job by the time he's twenty-two. He wants to become a musician, or maybe a songwriter. He isn't sure yet, but figures he has all the time in the world.

He grabs his controller and goes through to *Call of Duty*. Old, sure, but a classic, and destroying bratty twelve-year-olds is something he never gets sick of. He puts on his headphones, then takes a sip of his protein powder and leans back against the couch. In the freezer he has a frozen lasagna his mom made him, and he'll heat that up when he gets hungry, followed by some Halo Top.

A game begins, and his character runs forward. He spots his first enemy and aims, then gets a headshot.

"Cheater!" says a prepubescent voice through his headphones.

"Die mad," mutters Justin as he scratches his crotch.

The opposing team disconnects from the game, making the screen go black. The screen reflects Justin . . . and the masked figure creeping up behind him.

Justin yanks off his earphones and spins.

The intruder stops and tilts his head to the side. His mask is horrific: shiny hard plastic the color of faded bone, save for dark slashes of the eyes, and then a huge, curved grin for a mouth. There are no other features, giving the mask a sort of alien, inhuman quality, like a mannequin come to life. His clothes are all black: a leather jacket, black jeans, and combat boots, bulky enough to disguise whoever the person is under there. He's a monster from a horror story, made flesh.

He pulls a hunting knife from a pocket in his black jacket.

Justin raises his hands, taking slow steps backward to get away from the intruder. His mind struggles to process the horror that is in front of him.

"Who are you?" asks Justin. "What do you want?"

The killer lifts his hand and presses something on the side of his mask. A small red light turns on.

"Don't fight," says the figure. *"I'll make it quick."*

The voice is distorted to a higher pitch, disguising the speaker's real voice.

Justin keeps backtracking, his hands raised, until he finds himself backed all the way into the corner. He considers his options. He does have his phone in his pocket, but the masked freak is so close that he wouldn't be able to get help. Shouting won't get him help fast enough: Nobody else is home, and he is worried about startling whoever is under there into rushing forward.

"I can pay," he says. "Whatever you want, it's yours."

The killer advances, moving his knife from hand to hand.

"Hey, stop!" says Justin. "I'm warning you, I'll fuck you up."

"Try."

Justin sees his chance, and he charges to the side, jumps onto the couch, then springs over it, landing heavy but with a decent amount of distance between him and the killer. He runs for the front door, and makes it, and opens the door, but there's a second flyscreen. He sees the intruder behind him, then feels a blistering amount of pain in his back. He's been stabbed, he realizes with horrifying clarity.

The killer pulls out his knife with a wet squelching sound, making Justin gasp as pain spreads like wildfire from the wound. Justin strikes back with his elbow and hits the killer in the face, hard enough to make him stagger. Seeing his chance, Justin tries the door again, but he's too slow, and the killer swipes out. He ducks under the slash, and then makes a run for the stairs that lead to the second level of the house.

Justin runs up the steps and makes it to the top level before the man shoves him, pushing him to the wooden floor. He starts to crawl forward. His body feels weak and slow, and he isn't sure he has the energy to get to his feet right now. His gym shirt is soaking wet with blood.

The killer advances.

On display on the wall is his AΦN paddle that he got last year. The killer walks around Justin and unhooks the paddle from the wall. He admires it for a moment.

"Please," says Justin. Tears are streaming down his cheeks, and his perfect teeth are covered in blood. "Don't."

The figure brings the paddle up, and brings it down on Justin's face, knocking Justin's teeth out and pushing them to the back of the boy's throat. He chokes on shards of teeth as sharp as glass. The killer strikes him again, and again. Justin tries to bring his hands up, but he can't block the hits. Unbearable pain takes over everything.

He sees the figure pull the paddle back, getting ready to strike. Blood is splattered across his mask. The killer swings, and Justin braces himself.

The paddle connects, and everything goes black.

Chapter Eleven

"Cheers!"

We all bump our beers together, spilling some of the liquid out. I'm with Drew, Josh, and Booker, all with our new pledge pins on our chests. They're in the form of the fraternity coat of arms, a shield that has a tree, some stars, and a knight's helmet on it.

We're in the backyard of the frat house, and even though it's not that late yet, the party around us is already out of control. Hundreds of people are crammed into the backyard, dancing or talking. A Drake song is playing from the DJ booth, where a brother is DJing. Some people are already dancing, holding their red Solo cups up.

"Chug! Chug! Chug!"

I crack open the can and start to drink. Around me, all the other pledges are still drinking, so I keep going, and going, until I finish the can, the second of the night. The first is already starting to work, like fog slowly rolling over a hill.

"Good work, boys," says Tripp. "Grab your cans and come here."

Drew is the first to go up to him, holding his two cans. Tripp pulls a roll of Scotch tape from his pocket and binds the two cans together, before handing them back to Drew.

"Whoever's staff is the longest by the end of the night wins," says Tripp.

"Wins what?" asks Drew. He's even more of a lightweight than I am, as after only two drinks, he's starting to stagger.

"You'll see."

"What about whose staff is longest now?" asks Booker, wiggling his eyebrows. "Do I get any points for that?"

"We'll find out during hell week," says Tripp.

"Hell week?" I ask Josh, under my breath.

"It's the week before pledges are sworn in as brothers, and it's when the most intense testing happens."

"Like hazing?"

"Yeah. But they won't do that here," says Josh. "It'd get them kicked off campus."

With the guys I've met so far, I can't really see hazing being a thing. Even Tripp, who clearly loves partying and takes his role in the fraternity extremely seriously, doesn't seem the type to make me bend over so he can paddle me. It's my turn, so I step forward, and Tripp tapes my two cans together. I'm handed a fresh can, and then I go back to the others.

I crack open my beer and drink.

A short blond girl emerges from the crowd and kisses Tripp on the lips. She turns and spots me.

"You're Sam, right?"

"Yeah."

She sticks her hand out. "Beth Jones. I'm a fan."

A fan?

"Sorry, that was crass," she says. She reaches into her handbag and pulls out a business card. On it is the acid green logo for somethings called *Margaritas and Murder*—a podcast. Oh, I know. She must be a murder fan. "I'm a little starstruck."

"Not the time, babe," says Tripp.

"Right," says Beth. "Sorry. Anyway, if you ever want to be a guest, let me know. I'd love to have you on."

"I'll think about it."

"Perfect. I'll let you get back to it."

She kisses Tripp on the lips and goes back to the party. I put the card in my pocket, but there's no chance I'm ever going to take her up on that. No amount of money would be enough for me to ever go on a murder podcast.

"Sorry about that," says Tripp. "She's been waiting to meet you ever since you got here."

"It's all good."

I sip my beer. As a group, we migrate over to the beer pong table and join the crowd watching a game between some brothers and a group of sorority girls.

"Dude," says Drew, and he slings his arm over my shoulder. "Those girls are staring at you."

I look across the party at a group of Zeta Chi pledges, in pink shirts with Greek letters in silver across the front.

"So what?" I ask.

"They're hot," says Drew.

"You know I'm into guys, right?"

"Yeah, and that makes you the ideal wingman. Can you introduce me?"

I check again, and Drew is actually right: They are staring at me. Josh lifts his beer and takes a too-long drink.

"I thought you had a girlfriend," I say.

"Not anymore."

"Oh shit, man."

"It's all right."

Tears well up in his eyes, but he blinks them away.

"What happened?"

"I talked to her about how I was feeling, and she lost her shit and dumped me. It's for the best. We both knew long distance wasn't going to work."

"I'm sorry," I say.

"Don't be sorry. Introduce me to those girls."

I don't really think Drew needs a wingman, given how cute he is. But maybe I am overestimating his confidence.

With me leading the way, the four of us go over to the girls. Josh is already blushing and gripping the bottom of his staff so tight that the aluminum dents under his fingers. Booker seems the same as always, and Drew is standing up straighter.

"You're Sam Carville, right?" asks one of the sorority girls.

"Yeah."

"You're cuter than I thought you'd be."

"He's gay!" says Drew. "*Extremely* gay. Right, Carville?"

"Yep."

"No way," she says. "I love that for you. My brother's gay. You should meet him."

"Yeah, sounds good. This is my friend, D—"

"Did you get any scars or anything?"

"He has a pretty gnarly one on his chest," says Drew. "Go on, show them."

I shake my head.

"*Please,*" she says.

"Fine."

I pull down my shirt to show the scar on my chest. Then I switch my drink to my other hand and turn my arm to show them the long scar I have there.

"Wow," she says. "Did it hurt?"

It takes me a second to realize that was a serious question.

"Yeah."

"On a scale of one to ten, how bad was it?"

I try to hang on to some level of cool, because this is incredibly triggering. But this is a party, and I don't want to bring the mood down. Still, my skin crawls. How can someone be this casual about an attempted murder? Between this and Beth's podcast, it's a lot. I don't understand someone talking about murder so casually. If it's fiction, sure, but this really happened.

"Probably a ten," I say.

"I have a scar, too," says Booker, showing a thin line of scar tissue on the back of his hand. "I slipped while cutting up a pumpkin, but still. I'm Booker, by the way."

"Elise."

I start to zone them out, because across the party, something all sorts of amazing is happening. Oren is lying down on a table with his shirt pulled up, showing off his stomach. He has his hands behind his head and is beaming like this is the best night of his life. He lowers a hand and puts a wedge of lime into his mouth, then gets back into position. A brunette girl bends down and runs her tongue across the skin beside his navel, then takes a shot of something, and finally takes the lime out of Oren's mouth with her teeth. As she bites down, the crowd cheers.

"Who's next?" he calls, and he spots me looking. "Sam! Come here."

Before I can chicken out, I go up to Oren.

"They roped me into it," he says.

"Please," says a girl. "You know you want to."

"Fine, I guess I do."

She pours me a shot from a tequila bottle.

"I don't know," I say, taking a step back. "I'm already kind of drunk."

The crowd around us starts to chant for me to drink.

"You sure?" I ask Oren.

He lifts his shoulders, shrugging.

"Fine," I say, stepping forward. "What do I do?"

"Put some salt on my stomach, then take a shot, then grab the lime."

I'm handed the shot, and I grab the saltshaker. He lies back down, stretching out. I pour a line of salt onto his stomach, trying to ignore how perfect it is. He sticks the wedge of lime into his mouth. All right, here goes. I bend down and lick the salt off, and then take the shot. Oh God, it's disgusting. I finish it and then move forward, grab the wedge of lime with my teeth, being as careful as I can to not touch his lips, and bite down. The lime is better than the shot, which tastes like hand sanitizer, but combined, it's actually kind of awesome. The crowd cheers as I blink to get rid of the tears in my eyes.

Oren gets up off the table and pats me on the back. I'm still coughing, and my eyes are watering.

"You all right?" he asks.

I wipe the tears from my eyes. "I've never done tequila before."

"Do you like it?"

"It tastes like hand sanitizer."

"Fair. Here."

He hands me his drink, which is Coke and some kind of spirit. I take a drink, and it helps wash away the lingering taste of the tequila.

"Thanks," I say.

"You're welcome. By the way, you were the most requested little."

"Really?"

"Yeah. Everyone really likes you."

"That's awesome."

His eyes sparkle, and the whole party fades away, melting into irrelevance. He's wearing a light blue oxford shirt and chinos, and they fit him perfectly.

Oren's face falls. I see where he's looking. Mikey is standing by the entrance of the house, and he's clearly furious. He turns and storms off into the house.

"Sorry," I say.

"You haven't done anything wrong. He needs to grow up."

I agree. This has gone on far too long, and Mikey is, honestly, being a gigantic douche baby. To be this cut up over an ex feels so high school. If he doesn't want to be around Oren, then why doesn't he quit the frat? And what does he expect? This is college, and Oren is a hot single guy. He should be allowed to do whatever he wants without Mikey villainizing him, and we haven't really done anything. Sure, the body shot was hot, but it's hardly a major faux pas.

And again, Oren is single. He can do what he wants.

"Do you want a drink?" he asks.

"After getting the stink eye? Yeah, I think I'll need another."

As we walk, we bump into Brian.

"Have you seen Justin?" he asks.

I think about it. The party is crowded, but I haven't seen Justin.

"Nope," I say.

"I haven't, either."

"Weird. Keep an eye out for him, okay?"

"Will do," says Oren.

We go through to the kitchen, which has been trashed. The entire counter is covered in bottles and cups, and someone has left a lacy maroon bra on top of the fridge. I put my staff down.

Oren hands me a can that's maybe the brightest shade of neon I've ever seen. Ah. It's a Four Loko. I've heard of these and always thought they sounded like the sort of thing that could kill you. Judging from the amount of glee that is radiating from Oren now at the sheer prospect of me trying one of these, and from the radioactive brightness of the can, I'm going to go ahead and say that my initial assumption was correct. As he passes it to me, our fingers brush, and I feel sparks.

"He shouldn't have done that," says Oren.

I don't want to bad-mouth Mikey, so I keep my mouth shut.

"It's because you're cute," he says softly. "You're fit, and you've got really pretty eyes. Of course he's threatened."

I find myself starting to blush. I want to compliment Oren back: I could tell him he is fit and has pretty eyes, too, and yet, there is still this part of me that tells me I can't, because of Eli.

"Should he be?" I ask.

"What, threatened? Definitely."

I crack open the can and take a sip. Oh wow, yikes. It tastes like energy drink spiked with alcohol. A *lot* of alcohol. I'm not sure if whoever made this is a genius or an evil scientist, but it's most likely a mix of the two.

"Oh God," I say.

"Disgusting, right?"

"First tequila, now this?"

"I'm a bad influence."

"Clearly."

"Oren!" A girl is standing in the doorway to the kitchen. She's leaning on the doorframe, unmistakably wasted. Mascara runs down her cheeks, and her head keeps swaying. She hiccups, then turns to me. "Hello, handsome."

She slumps against the doorframe and closes her eyes.

"I should get her home," he says.

"Okay."

"I'll see you tomorrow, for Bloody Marys?"

I want to say it's a date, but I stop myself.

"Sounds good."

Chapter Twelve

Brian has always loved Dolly Parton.

His obsession with her started when he was a kid, and his interest surprised both his parents. While the other boys were playing with their monster trucks or Power Rangers, Brian was obsessively watching Dolly Parton videos on YouTube, bopping along to the beat, trying to mirror her. He even asked to go trick-or-treating as her one year, and now Brian's mom brings out those photos whenever she gets the chance, just to see how his face goes as red as the top and matching cowboy boots he wore.

He may no longer dress as her, but Dolly is still a comfort blanket for him. Her music soothes him and tells him everything will be okay. All it takes is one twang of her guitar playing in his mind and he's right back in his childhood living room, where nothing can hurt him.

He's in Toohey Park, walking along the pathway that leads back to his parents' house. During the day, this path is crowded: People jog or stroll while listening to music. Even though it's close to the campus, it feels a world away, as the trees block any view of the buildings.

Brian increases his pace. He doesn't want to be afraid; he is six feet tall and nearly two hundred pounds. If anyone attacks him, he can mess them up. But he's starting to freak himself out.

"'Working nine to five,'" he sings to himself under his breath. "'What a way to make a living.'"

He keeps his eyes peeled, ready to run at any sign of movement. Now that he's starting to sober up, he wishes he'd paid the $15.13 it would've cost to get a Lyft home. He told himself it was fine—he walks across Toohey Park all the time, and the campus is historically extremely safe. But fifteen dollars is a lot to him, and spending it would mean he'd need to be stricter on what food he buys, and what activities he says yes to. Most of his brothers have no idea how much little things cost, which he constantly finds infuriating. He doesn't have the luck of, say, Oren, with a lawyer father, or Tripp, whose mother is one of the most respected, and highly paid, surgeons in the country. It'd be nice, and maybe he'll be that rich one day, so his kid never has to walk through a park alone at night.

He passes under the glow of a streetlight. The next one up ahead isn't working, meaning the path isn't lit. He knows this path well, so he's aware he's about halfway home. The path makes a turn, then goes into a big open area of the park. It's so dark, though, that not much is visible outside of the areas lit by the streetlights.

Stupid, he thinks. *I'm never doing this again.*

Almost every night this week, he's been reading about what happened to Sam and his friends at the lake house, including reading *The Pleasant House.* It's scared him to the point where he has nightmares, often about monstrous creatures with constantly smiling faces ripping him to shreds, but he's kept going. Sam's going to be his brother soon, there's no way he's not going to make it through the pledging process. The brothers like to make it seem like it's really tough to make it, but it's actually not. As long as the pledge follows the rules and doesn't do anything egregiously wrong, then he will become a brother. Brian thinks it's his duty as a member of the brotherhood to know about Sam's past, to make sure that he is accommodated. Like, when Mikey suggested a horror movie night for all the pledges, Brian was the quickest to say that would be a bad idea, because of Sam. The guy has gone through enough; the last thing he needs is to go through something potentially triggering.

A branch snaps.

"Hello?" says Brian. His voice is strangled.

Nobody responds.

He crosses his arms and picks up his pace even more. It must be an animal or something. There's nobody out here. Even though *The Pleasant House* was inspired by real events, it's highly fictionalized. People like the Freak don't exist in real life. There are murders, but masked monsters? No way. That doesn't stop his imagination, though, and now every shadow is a masked killer. Brian reaches the faulty streetlamp and starts to run, not stopping until he reaches the light and perceived safety offered by the next one, which is working perfectly. He's in the deepest part of the park, and . . .

He stops, and an intense feeling of dread washes over him. He hasn't felt anything like it. It's all-consuming terror.

There's a masked figure standing on the path in front of him.

At first, Brian thinks it isn't real, that fear is messing with him, making him see things that aren't there. But that can only explain something for so long, and as the seconds pass, Brian realizes that this is real. His second thought is that this might be a prank—his brothers do play pranks all the time, and people know he's reading *The Pleasant House*. But none of his brothers would be this mean. There's no way. Wait. The mask this person is wearing . . . it's exactly the same as the one described in the book. That would mean he is looking at the Freak, made real.

He starts taking slow steps backward. He's not going to take any chances. The figure pulls a knife from the pocket of his leather jacket and steps closer.

"What do you want?" asks Brian. His voice is shaking.

The Freak takes a step forward.

Brian knows he needs to run.

"Help!" he shouts, and he turns and runs as fast as he can, back toward the frat house. "Help!"

Even drunk, he picks up speed. He ignores the pain in his lungs and thighs and keeps going. He looks over his shoulder, praying that the coast will be clear.

The man is right behind him. He's closed the gap effortlessly.

The Freak grabs Brian by the back of the shirt and pulls him into his awaiting blade. Brian gasps and feels a solid impact. For a split second he thinks he was punched, and then the pain comes on, exploding in his head with blinding whiteness, making him dizzy. The pain is like if someone has shoved a jagged spike right through his chest. The killer pulls out the knife just before Brian roars and swings around, lashing out with his fist. The Freak jumps back, then rushes forward, stabbing Brian in the stomach. Brian grabs on to him, and they fall together. They tumble over and over, down a grassy slope. They stop rolling, and Brian grabs the Freak's shirt and pulls him into a headbutt. The Freak recoils, stunned.

Brian shoves the Freak off and gets up. He staggers deeper into the park, until he is surrounded by thin trees. He doesn't dare look back. He reaches a tree and stops, pressing his back against it. He peers around and notices the Freak turning from side to side, searching for him. As quietly as he can, Brian lowers himself to the earth and curls his legs up. He can't run anymore, he doesn't have the energy. His shirt is wet and sticky, and a salty and metallic smell fills his nose.

He waits.

After a few minutes, he feels recovered enough to move. He gets up and starts running back toward the campus. He gets out of the thickest area of the park, and then . . .

He senses movement behind him, giving chase.

But it's too late for him. He's almost there, he can see the road.

He keeps running and then makes it out of the park, onto the road. A loud horn blares, and blaring whiteness fills his vision for a second before he sees a spinning tire coming right toward him.

Chapter Thirteen

My phone vibrates on my bedside table, waking me. I reach out and grab it. It's a message from Oren.

Where are you?

My room, why?

You should know something. Cops are looking for you.

What??

He leaves me on read. I push up off the bed and pace around my room. He still hasn't responded, so I text him again.

What happened?

I must still be dreaming. It's not real, it can't be. This has to be another nightmare, one I've had countless times before. Because this feels like the start of my worst fear, and that means the news I've spent the past two years trying to convince myself will never happen has finally become real.

I don't know that yet, maybe I'm jumping to conclusions. It wouldn't be the first time. Maybe there's some other reason why the cops would want to talk to me. I really freaking hope that there's another reason. I did drink underage last night, it could be about that. Or maybe something happened at the party that they want to talk to me about. Those hopes feel small, though, nothing but wishful thinking.

A heavy fist pounds on my door. I pull on the closest shirt and open the door.

Two police officers are standing in the doorway. One has short black hair and a floral sleeve of tattoos running down her right arm. The other has a sweet face, complete with a dimple in his cheek. Her name tag reads FUKUDA and his MCDOUGALL.

I can read what happened all over their faces. It's obvious.

Adrenaline flares through my body as the whole room gets brighter, and the world seems to narrow in on the two police officers standing outside my door, who have just confirmed that I was right. The entire time, I was correct. My nightmare wasn't over, I was just in a moment of peace. But the truth is I'm the star of a horror movie, and everyone knows what happens to them. The killer comes back, or someone decides to take up their mantle. It's what happens, always. The hair on my forearms and the back of my neck stands up, and a buzzing sound builds in my ears.

"I have something really difficult to tell you," says the first officer, Fukuda.

"Who?"

"It's Brian, Sam. He's gone."

I nearly drop to my knees. "What happened?"

"He was attacked in Toohey Park after the party. We think he was walking back to his parents' home and someone jumped him."

It all catches up to me. Brian is dead. It has to be because of me, because I came here. There's no other explanation that makes any sense. Someone killed Brian, and it has to be because of me.

"Is there someone you can talk to?" she asks.

"I'll call my dad."

I start to think it over and am confused. Why are they here? Surely they didn't feel the dire need to come here and tell me in person. From the sound of things, the killer is still out there. They have a job to do, so I have no freaking clue why they are here. None whatsoever.

"Would you mind coming to the station with us?" Fukuda asks.

"Why?"

I can't be a suspect, can I?

The pair share a glance.

"The killer left a message for you," says McDougall. He clears his throat. "With the body."

My mind races. It's all so much to process.

"Okay, give me a second."

"Take all the time you need," says Fukuda.

I close the door, and I picture Brian. I didn't know him

well—only talked to him maybe once or twice—but still. He was a person. He had a family and hopes and dreams, and all of that was taken away. All because of me.

I pull a pair of jeans over my boxers and put on some shoes. As I get dressed, I notice something outside, so I go over to my window and look out.

It's a circus.

There is media everywhere, all filming in front of my dorm. There must be at least a dozen different news vans, as well as a large crowd of students kept back by a barricade set up by the police. It's a frenzy out there.

And I'm going to have to walk through it.

I can't let myself panic. Brian was killed, and if his killer has a message for me, then I need to hear it. I can't hide from this, because the fact that the killer left a message for me means killing Brian wasn't his whole plan. It was just the beginning.

I stop for a moment and think of the lessons Dr. Patani taught me. Taking a moment to ground myself sometimes helps. Right now it doesn't help at all. I don't think anything will. This very fear has kept me awake for countless nights—that what happened at the lake wasn't the end of it. That, somehow, the nightmare would continue.

I go outside and the officers are still there.

"Ready?" asks Fukuda.

As I'll ever be.

I leave my room, locking it behind me. We take the elevator and go outside. The crowd sees me and starts to shout. Cameras flash. I can tell a bunch of cameras are pointed at me, and a few journalists rush forward, pointing microphones at my face. One of them is Beth, who is using her camera to film.

"Is he a suspect?"

"Sam, a word, please!"

"Killer!"

Everything stops. I look out and see that it's Mikey in the crowd, and he's the one who shouted that. Also among the crowd is Oren, who seems to be on the verge of tears. He can't believe what Mikey shouted, can he? He must know I didn't kill Brian.

"Stay back," says Officer McDougall. "Come on, Sam."

I put my head down and force my way through the huddle of reporters trying to block my path.

"Sam, one comment, please!"

"Did you know Brian?"

"Do you think this has anything to do with the Lake Priest murders?"

I pick up my pace, and we manage to reach a police station wagon. Fukuda opens the passenger-side door for me. Then she goes around to the other side and gets in, with McDougall getting into his own car a few yards away.

"Vultures," she says as she turns on the engine.

The crowd moves, and we drive off. Outside, the campus whips by. Brian's smiling face fills my mind.

He's dead.

I wish there was someplace I could go, some distraction I could use so that I can escape these thoughts. But there's nothing. I will never be able to escape this, and a part of me thinks that I never deserve to. Out the window I watch the campus pass by, and everything I see reminds me of him. This was Brian's home, and I decided to come here. I invaded his space, and now he's dead, because I decided I wanted a new life, even when I knew I didn't deserve it. The sickest part is that I'm not the one who paid for it—he did.

"It's going to be okay," says Fukuda.

I ignore her and keep looking out the window. I wish there was some way to make it so nobody says that word to me ever again, because nobody can ever promise that.

Don't cry, don't cry.

Soon we make it to the campus police station. I'm a zombie at this point. My entire self has been hollowed out. There's nothing left. Brian is dead because of me.

No, he's not just dead.

Someone killed him.

We leave the car and go inside. The receptionist stops what she was doing to openly stare at me from behind her desk. I let her. I am a sideshow; she may as well stare. We go into an interrogation room, which is just like the one after

Lake Priest. It's got plain walls, and what's clearly a two-way mirror. I wonder if anyone is on the other side, listening. Probably. I sit, keeping keep my head down, so I don't have to see my reflection.

"Wait here," says Officer Fukuda. "We'll be right back."

"Can I call my dad?"

"Good idea."

She leaves.

I take my phone out of my pocket and realize my hands are shaking. I call Dad.

I can barely speak, and even thinking about myself saying the words I need to makes my insides twist. What can I say? That my fear all along—that if I ever tried to live a normal life, this would happen—was founded?

"Hello," says Dad, his tone so cheery it's obvious that word hasn't reached him yet. Shit. That means that I need to be the one who tells him what happened. "How's campus life going?"

"I have to tell you something."

"Okay, what?"

"A boy was killed last night. Brian."

Dad goes silent.

"I'm at the police station now." Tears brim in my eyes. "Can you come get me?"

"Of course, I'm on my way."

I hear him pick up his keys, so I know he means it. He

will be here as fast as possible. Someone knocks on the door to the room.

"Gotta go," I say.

"Sam, wait . . ."

"I'll see you soon."

I hang up.

"Come in," I call.

The two officers, Fukuda and McDougall, come into the room. Fukuda is now holding a plain folder. This must be what she wants to show me. The message from the killer. I don't know if I'm ready for that. The fact it exists confirms that my darkest thoughts are the cold hard truth: Someone killed Brian because of me.

The officers sit down.

"I want to give you a warning," says Fukuda, her fingertips tapping against the folder on the table. "This isn't easy to look at."

"Show me."

"Are you sure?" asks McDougall. "Think about it. It's not the sort of thing you can forget."

"Just show me."

She opens it.

The picture is of Brian's body in a morgue. He's facedown. It's him, though. My name has been carved into his back: *SAM*. The letters are big and bloody, but there's no blood around the slashes. I'm no expert, but I assume that means the killer made the carvings when Brian was dead, or maybe he cleaned the blood off to make sure there was no missing his message.

"We have some camera footage," she says. "The killer wore a mask, but he took it off farther down the park. We're hoping you can help us identify him."

"Okay."

She turns to the next page in the folder, and there are some printed black-and-white photos. In one, the killer is standing over Brian's body. My breath catches. That mask . . . it's the Freak's mask. He's wearing the mask of the killer in *The Pleasant House*. Whoever this monster is, he was inspired by my mom's book.

Fukuda turns the page.

"Do you recognize this man?" asks Fukuda.

He has longer hair, and he's definitely aged. But there's no mistaking who it is.

It's Eli.

Chapter Fourteen

Can I get you anything?" asks Dad.

I'm looking at him through the crack in my doorway at Peter's place. I guess I should feel self-conscious, because I haven't showered in two days and I definitely smell terrible. I've barely left my room, barely even moved—but I don't have the energy for that. I don't have the energy for anything, and I don't even care. I've grown some stubble, and there are giant bags under my eyes, and even then I'm not sure I look as terrible as I feel. That would be impossible.

I shake my head.

"You should eat," says Dad.

"I'm not hungry."

My room is dark, lit only by the lamp on my bedside table. It's not really *my* room. It's my room in Peter's house, where I'm going to be for the foreseeable future. I can't go back to Munroe, I can't get a job, because they all involve other people, I can't leave, so this is it for me. Just me in this shitty room in this shitty house with shitty fucking Peter.

It's clear now that I got ahead of myself, wanted things I could never have. I can't have a normal life.

Two people are dead because of me.

Justin's body is missing, but there was enough blood at the scene of the crime to know he passed. Dad had to tell me, after he got a call. They didn't really need to tell him, as it's all the news is talking about right now. I just nodded and asked to be left alone. I could tell that Dad didn't want to leave me, but I didn't really give him a choice.

Brian and Justin are dead because I tried to be someone I'm not. I will never, ever get to be normal.

"Can I come in?" asks Dad.

I open the door a little more and sit down on my bed. I want to open the blinds and get some air, but that might mean exposing myself. Paparazzi and news crews have been camped out on the front lawn ever since I got home, hoping to get a proper look at me. It's pretty wild to me that they aren't breaking the law, that they can harass us like this and it's totally fine, as long as they don't step foot on our property. After news spread that a killer attacked the college that I was attending, in a costume inspired by my mom's book, the story blew up. It's worldwide now, and I'm more famous than I've ever been. People say I'm cursed . . . or that I'm the killer. People on Reddit are having a grand time speculating about my apparent breakdown and turn for the murderous.

I'm the most obvious suspect, apparently. Armchair detectives have flooded my social media with comments calling me a murderer so much I put them on private.

"Sorry it's so messy," I say. "I should've cleaned."

"It's not that bad."

It's a lie, but I'll let it slide. I can't really hold anyone accountable for anything, not after what I've done. Dad closes the door behind him and locks all the locks. He sits down beside me.

There is a manhunt for Eli underway, but so far, no luck. I know they won't find him. He won't make it that easy, and he would've planned this whole thing out. He wouldn't start and end the killings with Justin and Brian, two people I had met but barely new. Those two are just the start. He'll move to someone closer to me soon, I know. And me? He'll save me for last, only killing me once I've suffered enough.

"I think you should talk to Dr. Patani," says Dad. "She can help."

"I don't want to."

"Why not?"

"I just don't."

We both go quiet.

"What happened isn't your fault."

I don't say anything.

"It's not," says Dad.

"What do you want me to say?"

"For you to listen. This is *not* your fault."

"But it is. Brian and Justin wouldn't be dead if it weren't for me. Eli killed them, Dad. If I'd picked any other school, they would be fine. They're dead because of me. What if . . ."

"What if what?"

"What if I knew this would happen?"

Dad's eyes widen a fraction. "What do you mean?"

"There's this part of me that knew something like this would happen again one day. I was right."

"No." Dad is trembling with anger now, and I don't think I've ever seen this from him. "Stop talking like this."

"Can you go?" I ask. I lie down, so I'm facing my wall and my back is to him. "I want to go back to bed."

"It's not even five, and you haven't eaten anything all day. I can make you a smoothie or something."

For some reason, it sets me on edge. Maybe making smoothies can fix the problems that Dad has come up against in life, but he has no idea about the shit that I have to go through. He has no idea how this feels. He has no idea how every single second feels like my insides are being shredded.

"Can you please leave me alone?"

"Okay. I'm going."

"Make sure Peter doesn't accidentally leave a door or window unlocked."

Dad stops in the doorway, clearly at a loss as to what to do. Which I understand—I'm at a loss, too. I don't know how I can keep on living knowing what I've done, what I did to two perfectly normal, innocent boys.

When Dad leaves, I lock the door, then do up the three additional locks. Next I check the window, making sure it's locked tight. Once I'm sure everything is secure, I pull the blinds closed and sit on the end of my bed.

I picture Justin and Brian. And Eli.

He's a murderer. I've killed someone, too, but that is different. That was self-defense, and the person I killed was most assuredly not innocent. I killed him because I had to. Eli killed two people because . . . I guess I don't know, and that uncertainty makes me want to cry. Even if I don't think I deserve it. That guilt wipes away the urge to cry, replacing it with a dull sadness.

A part of me wishes Eli had killed me instead. I don't want to die, but Justin and Brian died because of me. It's so unfair.

An hour later, my phone vibrates. I grab it, and it's a message from Oren.

Hey, just checking in. I'm here if you want to talk.

At least he didn't promise me anything that he can't.

I lock my phone and roll back over so I'm facing the wall.

I can't eat.

I'm sitting at the dinner table, moving a piece of chicken

around my plate without eating it. This is the first time I've left my room in hours, and I'm mostly here for Dad and Gus's benefit rather than my own. Peter has made a ridiculously over-the-top feast: a roast chicken, baked macaroni and cheese, roasted vegetables, and gravy made from scratch. It's as if we have something to celebrate. There's even an apple pie in the oven, baking. Nobody is really hungry, though, not even Gus, and he eats constantly. I hate that we're even going through the motions of this for *Peter's* benefit. Sure, I get that cooking is his way of coping, but why do we need to entertain him?

"How was work?" asks Dad.

"Good," says Peter as he hacks into his chicken. "Busy."

"Why was it busy?"

"I was fully booked, mostly checkups, and Noel came in for her final Invisalign appointment, which was exciting."

Who gives a flying fuck? Surely Dad doesn't actually care about the riveting adventure of someone called Noel's Invisalign.

No, we're all thinking about what happened to the boys at Munroe and how I'm responsible. We're trying to pretend otherwise, which means this whole dinner is a joke.

I check my phone, and there are no new messages. Josh, Booker, and Drew have each messaged me a few times, and Tripp and Alyson checked in once, but that's been it, aside from Oren's first message, which I haven't replied to. Mom hasn't messaged me, and neither has Eli. I wish I didn't want a message from Mom, but I do. She probably loves this. Why come up with her own story line when I can go through hell to inspire her? I bet her publisher has already been in contact.

Peter looks up at me. "How are you?"

"How do you think?"

"I don't know—that's why I asked."

"Shut up, Peter."

"*Sam.*"

I know I'm about to get sent from the table, so I storm off and go upstairs. In my bedroom, I lock all my locks and check everywhere someone could be hiding, and when everywhere turns out to be clear, I drop down onto my bed. I flip over and punch my pillow as hard as I can.

I get out of bed and sit down at my computer. I go straight to the news articles on the case and scroll the headlines.

MUNROE STUDENTS KILLED IN BRUTAL SLAYINGS

MASKED KILLER DESCENDS ON MUNROE

RUTHLESS SLAYINGS OF TWO TEENAGE STUDENTS LEAVE PRESTIGIOUS UNIVERSITY SHAKEN

Fukuda was right. Journalists are vultures.

In a way, the people reading are as bad. I can picture it

now, people all over the country using Brian's and Justin's deaths to feel something, because they're so hollowed out they need something violent and tragic to happen for them to have any kind of emotional reaction. I honestly don't think I'll ever get why some people like to read about this stuff. Maybe people who feel superior because they don't drink to excess, like Brian did, because he wouldn't be dead if he had been sober. Justin apparently left his front door unlocked, and I made the mistake of reading comments, lots of which called Justin, a dead teenage boy, stupid. People say Brian deserved what happened to him because he was drunk underage, or a frat boy.

Maybe Oren will be the good type of journalist. I hope so, because these people are awful.

I click on the top link.

MUNROE STUDENTS KILLED IN BRUTAL SLAYINGS

Nineteen-year-olds Brian Collins and Justin Lynch were murdered late last night by an unknown assailant. Justin was murdered in his home, and Brian was killed while walking home from a rush week party at the historic Alpha Phi Nu fraternity.

"It's important for students to be careful," said Joseph Morris, dean of students at Munroe University. "Especially until we can find who is responsible. Classes are suspended for the week, and counselors are available to all students. When classes resume, we encourage students to be careful, especially at night."

> "They were the best guys," said Neil Tripp, president of Alpha Phi Nu, where Brian and Justin were brothers. "They were so excited for the term and were eager to get to know all the new pledges better."

Tears sting in my eyes.

I load the next article. MASKED KILLER DESCENDS ON MUNROE.

Looking at these is like picking at a scab. It doesn't help, it just makes everything worse, but I can't help myself; it's a sick compulsion. I'm flogging myself in the back and pouring salt into the wounds. Maybe I can't change what happened, but I can hurt myself. I guess that makes me feel like I'm doing something.

After I read the article, I go to Justin's Facebook, which has been changed to a memorial. And I pick. I pick, I pick. I read long, heartfelt messages from his family, all talking about what a stand-up guy Justin was. Most mention what a big future he should've had, which he was robbed of. More than one person said he was going to change the world. It's hard to argue with them. Who knows what he could've achieved if he had lived to a mature age? He could've done anything if it weren't for me.

A fly is crawling on top of a lumpy bowl of uneaten pasta beside me. I scoop up the bowl, and the fly escapes. I dump the gluggy contents into my trash can, then grab a can of fly spray from my drawer. I walk around and find the bastard crawling along my window, trying to get out. I open the window, letting it escape.

There's nobody on the front lawn. All the reporters have left.

I open my blinds and push the window farther up, letting in some fresh air. Then I go back to my computer and pick again: I go to Mom's Twitter.

Her banner, *The Pleasant House—Based on a true story,* from the cover of her novel, haunts me yet again. I mean, it's the last book she released, so I kind of get it, but still. She's retweeted a few articles about the murders, and the general chaos at Munroe, and has liked a bunch of messages asking her if she is going to write a sequel now. I know Mom enough to know that she must be thinking about it, at the very least—if people are asking to read something she's written, she's powerless to resist. She'll give in, no matter the cost, no matter if it makes her look like an asshole. Clearly she has had enough time to check Twitter but not enough time to message me.

A knock sounds on my door. I switch tabs, close my laptop.

"What?" I call.

"It's me," says Peter through the door. "Can I come in?"

I close my eyes and then start unlatching my locks. Once they're all undone, I open the door a crack. I feel all the hate and resentment toward Peter that I usually do, but I have to push that down. I was an asshole at dinner, and it hasn't done anything other than make me feel worse.

"I'm sorry I told you to shut up," I say.

He waves a hand. "Can I come in?"

I open the door wider, and Peter walks in and looks around my room. If I cared what he thought of me, I guess I would feel judged at how much mess is strewn around anywhere.

"We should have a drink," says Peter. "Do you want to?"

"Sure."

Peter and I go down to the kitchen. There's clearly something he wants to tell me, as he's got nervous energy radiating off him.

"What is it?" I ask.

He pulls down two scotch glasses from a cabinet above the fridge and places them on the table.

"I'd like to fix things between us. Your outburst at dinner . . . I think you've been holding it in for a while, and I want you to talk to me."

"I don't know what to say."

"Let's start with: Why don't you like me?"

We've never spoken this honestly with each other. I wasn't expecting him to go for the jugular like this, and now a slow-motion car wreck is happening, and I know the point of lying to salvage it has passed, because I have taken too long, and now he knows what I really feel. I see it sink in, with hurt settling in his eyes.

"Right," he says, nodding. "So you don't like me."

"You're a grown man, you shouldn't be asking if I like you or not."

"See, there it is. The resentment. Is it because your dad isn't with your mom anymore?"

"No, he should've ended that a long time ago," I say.

"Is it because I'm Black? Or a man?"

"No, of course not."

"I'm just checking," he says.

"It's just . . . sometimes I don't really believe you think things through enough, and I find it so annoying."

"Okay, so I'm careless?"

"No, it's that when you talk to me, you don't seem to think about what you say."

"And that annoys you?"

"A lot, yeah. You are right, though. I've been a dick to you, and I really shouldn't have been. You haven't done anything wrong."

"I'm happy to hear that."

His eyes are glassy, and I don't think he's acting. I think he really does deeply care about how I feel about him. And it's hard to be mad at someone when they're showing this much unfiltered emotion. It's also possible that I'm the one in the wrong here, and I have been petty and juvenile, which, shockingly, are two things I don't want to be.

"I guess a part of me is scared," I admit.

"Of what?"

"You didn't see what Dad was like when things were ending with Mom. He was devastated."

"Are you scared I'll hurt him?"

I suck in a breath. "Yeah."

"I'm not going to."

"You can't promise that. It doesn't mean anything."

"You're right. I can't control what will happen in the future—that's impossible. But I can promise I'm going to try to the best of my ability to make him happy."

"I believe you."

"That's a start." He twists open the bottle. "I never thought I'd feel how I feel about you and Gus."

"And how's that?"

"I know I'm not your parent, and I'm not saying it's the same, but I feel very protective of you two. I'm a gay man; I spent my twenties and thirties casually dating. I never thought I'd want anything serious. And then I met your dad and this switch flipped, and now all I want is to keep the three of you safe."

"That's going to be harder with me than it is with the others."

That gets him to smile. "I'm up for it."

Peter pours one scotch and hands it to me. He pours one for himself, then lifts his glass.

"Truce," he says.

I bang my glass against his.

Chapter Fifteen

"Sam," calls Dad from outside my door.

The fact that he's here is weird. He should be at work right now, because it's just past nine in the morning. I didn't ask him to, but I guess he decided to stay home to look after me. I wish I wasn't grateful, because I've already been so disruptive to his life already, but I can't help it. It's the morning after I made my truce with Peter, and I wasn't planning on leaving my room at all. Even a single second out of bed is torturous.

I unlatch my locks and open the door a little.

"You need to see something," he says.

I go down into the kitchen. There is a large package sitting on the kitchen island. Peter is standing behind it, eyeing it warily, his arms crossed. I'm already feeling closer to Peter than I ever have. Normally the sight of him sets me on edge, but this time, I actually feel something close to affection. Weird.

It looks as if it's an ordinary parcel, but it could be anything.

"This was at our front door," says Dad. "It's addressed to you. We talked about not showing you, but I thought you deserved to see it."

I realize now why both of them look so freaked out. This parcel, whatever it is . . . it's from Eli. It's a clear message. Eli knows where we live. This is a threat.

I grab a knife and start cutting open the tape.

Inside, the box is filled with the severed heads of piles of male dolls. I dig around in the box, but there's nothing there. Just a slew of doll heads. Each one has the same facial features; the only difference is the color of their hair.

"Why would he send this?" asks Peter.

I glance at Dad. I also wonder if he knows.

"It's a threat," I say.

Dad takes his phone out of his pocket.

"What are you doing?" I ask.

"Calling the cops. You can go back to bed; we'll handle this."

A part of me wants to fight, to say that this mess is happening because of me, so I'm the one who should follow through. I don't have the energy, though. I'm so tired, and I can't bring myself to stay here. Not with this. Because I don't really have any other options, save for making Dad, Peter, and Gus hunker down until Eli is caught. Gus stayed home from school today, and that was the right call. I don't think Dad, Peter, or Gus should leave the house at the moment—it's way too dangerous.

"All right."

I go back up the stairs. Now I'm picturing Dad with his head cut off, just like the dolls. His neck is a bloody stump, trickling blood.

I think there was more to the message than Eli simply telling me he knows where we live. There is a reason the box was filled with the heads of men. He killed two of my fraternity brothers, and I think this is a message that he will kill more. Is that what he's trying to express? That more of my brothers will die?

I go to my room, and sit at my computer, and I get an idea.

I go through the contacts list on my phone and find Eli's number. The last time I messaged him was last year.

I write him a text.

I got your message. As soon as you get this, call me.

Buzzt.

Buzzt.

I open my eyes warily. The phone is sitting faceup on my bedside table and is letting off blue light. I was dozing, even though it's not even 1:00 P.M. I did manage to slip into some restless sleep, during which I'm pretty sure I was hunted by the Freak in my dreams. I grab my phone and flinch at the name on the screen.

Eli is calling me.

I watch it ring before grabbing it and swiping to accept the call.

"Hello?"

"Hello, Sam."

His voice is being changed by some sort of program to raise the pitch, so it doesn't sound like Eli. It barely sounds human. But it is him. Fukuda caught him on camera—he is the Freak. He is the one who murdered Brian and Justin and sent a box full of doll heads to Peter's house. I am talking to a cold-blooded murderer. My mind struggles to process that they are the same person, because it tells me that's impossible.

"Why are you doing this?" I ask.

"I'm not going to tell you that."

"Why not?"

"Figuring it out is part of the fun."

"I don't want to have fun with you, you sick bastard. You need to turn yourself in."

"And you need to come back to Munroe."

"Why would I do that?"

"Because I asked nicely."

"You're sick. You need help."

"Shh. There are so many handsome boys on campus, don't you think?"

I grip my phone tighter. "You're doing this because you're jealous? You need help."

"I make the rules, do you understand?"

"I do."

"Every day you're not here, I will kill one boy. I don't care what they do, nothing will stop me. I'll find them and rip their guts out, and it will be your fault."

"Eli, please . . ."

"You can stop it, though. If you come back to campus today and follow my rules, I won't hurt anyone else."

"Why should I believe you?" I ask.

"Have I ever lied to you?"

"No. Why are you hurting them? They didn't do anything to you."

"Because it's the best way to hurt you."

"Why do you want to hurt me?"

"I want to kill you, Sam. But you knew that already, didn't you?"

"You need help."

"You have until midnight tomorrow."

The line goes dead.

Chapter Sixteen

"Sam?"

It's Gus, his quiet voice coming from outside my room. Under the door, I can see the shadows from his feet. Yesterday the cops came by to collect the box that Eli sent. I stayed in my room when they came over.

It's early in the morning, I'd guess about five, which is definitely way earlier than Gus normally wakes up. If he had it his way, I'd bet that he would sleep all day and stay up all night. I was exactly the same when I was a kid, and even if I am less of a night owl now, I remember it well.

I unlock my door, and Gus comes in.

"Are you okay?" he asks.

I sit in my computer chair and close the window I have open, which displays a news article about the murders. "I am."

"I'm not a kid anymore," he says. "You don't have to lie to me."

I mean, he most definitely is still a kid. But he's right. I shouldn't lie to him. I can be honest with him without telling him all the gory details of my PTSD.

"You're right," I say. "I'm sorry."

"It's okay." He swings his arms. "What should I do if he attacks me?"

"You're safe here."

"You said you were safe at Munroe."

"I did. But that's different."

"Why?"

"I guess it isn't."

He smiles and tilts his head up, impressed with himself. And I have to say, he should be, because damn is it hard to argue with his logic right now.

"Okay," I say, and I open my bedside drawer and pull out a Taser.

Gus fixes his gaze on it, his jaw slightly slack. "Dad says I can't touch those."

"I know, but I want to show you how they work, okay?" I hand it over. "Be careful."

"Can these kill someone?"

"It's designed to stun, not kill."

"A gun would be better."

"Do you know how to shoot a gun?"

"No."

"Then you shouldn't have one. If someone attacks you, jam it into them and then press this button, and zap."

"Can I try it?"

"Sure."

I show him the button on the side, and he presses it. The end gives off a tiny electrical sound.

"Wicked," he says. "So I stun them; then what?"

"Run."

He turns the Taser over in his small hands. I wish he didn't have to know this, because he's eight years old. That's way too little to need to know about killers and Tasers.

"Can I keep it?" he asks. "I know you have spares."

I start to say no, but then I stop myself. Dad has said that Gus can't touch these, but that was before. If Eli is out there wanting to make me suffer, then there is one huge target that he would go for: the person I can't live without.

"It's yours," I say.

Dad is in the kitchen, making himself a bowl of muesli. Just plain muesli, without any weird herbs or supplements. It's how I know something is up, because he's still acting so infuriatingly normal.

We should be safe inside, because I've triple-checked every entryway and security panel. All the batteries and locks work properly. There's no way that Eli is getting into this house.

After Eli hung up, I spent the entire night thinking, trying to figure out what the best possible move is—listening to him feels like a mistake, but the thing is, I know his threat isn't a bluff. If I don't listen to him, he will kill again. I know he'll keep his word, which means I have to go back.

But first, I need to tell Dad. I've been trying to muster up the courage to say the words to Dad for the past hour since I got up, but keep bailing. He's going to try to stop me, because even with Eli's threat, I'm still safest here. I'm running out of time, and I think Eli will keep his word. If going back can slow Eli down by even a few hours, then it will be completely worth it. Even if it means I get attacked by the Freak.

All right, here goes nothing.

"I want to go back to campus," I blurt.

Dad lowers his spoon and stares at me. From his reaction, it's as if I've just told him something totally bizarre. "You're joking, right?"

His eyebrows twitch, and I can see the cogs working in his mind. Then, light bulb.

"Did Eli call you?" he asks.

"No."

"Don't lie, Sam."

"I'm not."

"Yes, you are! I've raised you for eighteen years, I know when you're lying. What did he say?"

"Nothing. I can't stay here anymore, Dad."

There's a chance Dad is right. He's only looking out for

me, and if it was Gus who had come to me asking if it was okay for him to throw himself in danger, then I would put my foot down. Hard. And maybe it is the best move to stay here and wait this out. The cops will be able to find Eli, and once that happens, I can go back.

The faces of the people I met fill my mind. Oren. Josh. Booker. Drew. Everyone I even came into slight contact with is in danger. If I stay here, the Freak will attack one of them. That means I need to act my ass off now, because there is only one angle I can use that Dad would accept enough to let me go back to campus.

"Why?" he asks.

"Because I want a life! And I want you to have one, too. And Gus. If I stay here, I'm making everything worse."

"You're not making anything worse. Please, think this through."

"I have, and I've—I've made my decision. I'm going."

"It's not safe."

"Nowhere is safe," I say, raising my voice. "Not for me. Do you want him coming here? He could attack you, or Gus, and I can't stop him."

"I'm not letting you put yourself in danger for us; that's not your decision."

"I'm not. I'm just going back to campus. I got a mass email from the dean, and he said it's safe because they've increased security and set a curfew."

"No."

"What do you mean, no?"

"It's not safe," he says. "We'll move, and put this all behind us."

Impossible.

"I'm not asking, I'm telling. I'm sick of hiding, and I'm going back."

Dad's pointer finger taps on his biceps, a nervous twitch of his whenever he is thinking really hard about something.

"I can't stop you," he says. "But please, don't do this."

"I'm sorry, I have to."

"When will you go?"

"Now. I'll get the bus."

"I'll drive you. You're not going to take any chances, okay?"

Finally, a promise I know I can keep.

Chapter Seventeen

I'm trying to feel the way that I did when I first arrived at Munroe.

I can remember the excitement, the anxiety, the level of anticipation that was nearly out of control. I want to feel that way again, but I know I can't. Munroe used to be untouched, my chance for a new life. Now it's more of the same, as tainted by my past as almost everything in my life has been. This whole drive has been weird, to put it lightly. Dad clearly doesn't want me to go back to campus, but he's forcing himself not to say anything. We've barely spoken. All we've been doing is listening to the radio, which is playing a bunch of identical-sounding pop songs, each one blandly safe. It's probably misplaced aggression, but each one is pissing me off to an almost extreme degree. Who decided that people can make millions of dollars producing songs that sound like this?

I glance at Dad. He's gripping the steering wheel tight, and I swear he's driving slower than he normally does. I've never gone against him like this. I know it's what I have to do, though. Nobody else is going to die because of me.

"What are you thinking about?" asks Dad.

"Nothing."

He huffs but returns his attention to the road.

We reach the Munroe sign and pass by it without comment. We make it to my dorm, and Dad pulls off the road. The campus is different. When I was here last time, it was buzzing with activity. Now it's still, and so quiet. Too quiet. I know from the email the dean sent that the first week of classes has been pushed back to next week, but seeing it in real life is something else.

"Thanks for driving," I say.

He puts the car in park and undoes his seat belt.

"What are you doing?"

"I'm walking you to your door. Do you have your Taser?"

I take it out and show him.

Inside, my dorm building is pretty similar to what it is like outside: It's much quieter than it should be. This should be the first week of classes; everyone should be here. The only reason classes have been delayed is because of me. We go up the elevator. I readjust my grip on the Taser, and we head down the hall.

We reach my door without incident. I unlock my door and then check all the hiding spots. When we find there's nobody in here, I pocket my weapon.

"Is there any way I can talk you out of this?" Dad asks.

I shake my head. "I'm sorry."

"Just be smart, okay? If I lost you, I don't know what I'd do."

"I'll be fine."

Dad hugs me, squeezing me tight. "Don't do anything stupid, all right?"

"I won't."

"Don't go out alone at night. If you want to go anywhere, pay someone to drive."

"I will."

"I'll pay, no matter how much it costs." He hugs me again. "Is there *anything* I can do to convince you to come back home with me?"

"Nope."

"Okay. If it takes you longer than half an hour to respond to a text, I'm calling the cops."

"Sounds good."

"Okay. I'll call you when I get home."

"All right."

He leaves. I close my door, then take out my phone and text Eli.

I'm here.

I know, I saw.

Hey, I just got back to campus. Are you around?

I have the message saved, ready to send to Josh. I haven't been able to hit send yet. What if he doesn't want to see me anymore? I would get it, too. I want to talk to him, though. He likes horror movies, so he might have an idea of how to catch Eli so all of this can end.

And honestly, I don't want to be alone right now. Maybe if we can hang out like we did during rush, then I wouldn't feel like this.

I hit send, then toss my phone away so it lands on my bed.

That was stupid. There's no way that he's going to want to spend time with me, not after two people died because of me. Maybe I should have just . . .

Bzzt.

Josh has responded.

Hey, man! I'm sorry, I left campus, it didn't seem safe. Drew and Booker are still around, if you need someone to talk to.

Oh.

This is damning.

It's a good move—getting himself away from me is probably the best way for him to stay safe.

My room suddenly feels so quiet.

All I can do is wait until Eli messages me. I don't have any classes to distract myself, or any fraternity things, because those have all been put on hold as well. My pledge pin is still sitting on my dresser. I pick it up and admire it. In another life, I'd be having the best time as a pledge. I'd be spending as much time as I possibly could with Oren, and I'd hang out with the other pledges. It would be amazing. I might even be fixing things with Alyson, not ghosting her yet again.

I swipe through on my phone, and I feel curious, so I go to Beth's podcast. She's uploaded a new episode, titled "Murders at Munroe."

I hit play.

"Hey, welcome to *Margaritas and Murder*. I'm Beth, and I love murder. This week's episode is a big one, folks, and one I know you've been dying to hear me talk about. That's right, I'm going to talk about the murders of Brian Collins and Justin Lynch, two young men I had the honor of knowing myself. I'm going to give you a front-row seat to what happened. I've had a lot of people tell me I should leave to stay safe, but don't worry, I'm going to be fine. I've got pepper spray and my whistle. Plus, let's say I'm not the kind of person the killer is interested in."

My phone chimes.

It's a text from Oren.

Hey, I heard you got back to campus. Want to grab a coffee?

I know I should say no. It's the safest thing for him. Yet there's still that dream I have of what this year should be. Spending time with Oren is a big part of that, and here is my chance. I run through potential risks, and it should be fine. It's the middle of the day, which isn't Eli's MO. As long as we go somewhere that's well lit and has plenty of people, and we don't make a decision to go somewhere private, then it will be fine.

Somewhere public?

Great. The Grove in half an hour?

I'll see you then.

The biggest Munroe coffee shop, the Grove, is split over two levels, with booths running along the far walls and loads of tables, almost all of which are empty right now. I can picture what this would look like while classes are on: People would be in here on their laptops, chugging iced coffees in order to power through their assignments or to study before their exams. Right now there's just a girl with messy hair reading a YA novel with a bluish-green cover about someone called Leah, and a pair of people focused on their computers.

"Grab us a table?" asks Oren. "And what would you like?"

"I can get it."

"My shout. You can get the next one."

His eyebrows lift up. "Sorry, um, I shouldn't have said that."

"No, it's fine, I'll owe you. A cappuccino, please, with oat."

"That's my order," he says as he makes eye contact.

"Seriously?"

"Yep."

I go to an empty booth with a good view of the front door and slide in. I check my phone, and I haven't gotten any new messages from Eli. That's a good thing, at least. I have followed his instructions, and he managed to get me back here, but at the same time I don't really believe that. He asked me back here for a reason, so there's no way that he will just leave and give up. No, if things have gone quiet it's because he's waiting for the right time to strike.

Oren comes back holding two plates, each with an enormous chocolate cookie. They seem homemade, and my guess is that they are more chocolate than cookie, which is my favorite ratio when it comes to cookies.

"They looked too good to resist," he says as he places the cookie down in front of me. Faint lines of steam are rising up from it, and the chunks of chocolate are melted and gooey. My mouth starts to water, and I'm struck by how sweet it is that he got this for me. I think I needed it more than he knows.

"You're welcome," he says.

He smiles, and my God, is his smile cute. It's a little lopsided. Even with everything going on, it's impossible to miss how cute it is. How cute he is, really. As he has been every time that I have seen him, he's wearing a great outfit, and his skin is almost flawless. He doesn't even have any bags under his eyes, like he hasn't missed a second of sleep. He must have, because there's no way he hasn't, but he's somehow found a way to hide it. Now isn't the time, but at some point, I should ask him about his routine.

"How are you feeling?" he asks.

"I'll be okay."

"I know, that's not what I asked."

"Right," I say. "I'm scared."

"Me too."

"Guilty . . . ," I continue.

"Guilty?"

"Yeah."

"Why guilty?"

Tears fill my eyes. I can't help them, even if it's not fair of me to cry. Oren has lost two of his friends, and it's my fault. He should be the one venting to me, not the other way around. And yet, I appreciate what he is doing for me so much. This is like when I was offered a beer at the first rush event that I went to. Over the past two years I've been sure that people would dislike me if they found out what I've done, and recently I've been convinced that the brothers would be the same as the people on the internet and would blame me.

That fear seems unfounded, though.

"This isn't your fault," he says. "You know that, right?"

"It kind of is."

"No, it's not."

"This wouldn't have happened if I didn't come here."

A waiter comes over and places two coffees down in front of us. I glance at the waiter, and I see recognition in his eyes, which is quickly replaced by fear. He goes back to the coffee machine, and it might just be in my head, but it seems like he got away from me as fast as he could.

"Listen to me," says Oren. "You aren't to blame for this."

"You know about the lake."

He blinks. "I do, yeah."

"Do you know what I did?"

He watches me, his gaze steady. "I do. What does that have to do with anything?"

I want to tell him that it means I'm a bad person. And that this feels like some sort of cosmic retribution, a way for the scales to rebalance. You can't kill someone without some sort of cost.

"I don't know."

"I knew Brian and Justin," says Oren. "They were my brothers. And they wouldn't blame you."

"Really?"

"I know they wouldn't. This isn't your fault."

All right. That's two people who have told me that now. Maybe I should listen. I think about it, if my past had happened to Oren, and then this happened. It's pretty clear that

I wouldn't blame him, I would blame Eli. I can extend that same grace to myself. It feels a little wrong, like I don't really deserve it. I can try to ignore that feeling, though. I've gotten pretty good at that.

"Thanks," I say. "I needed to hear that."

"Anytime."

I take a bite of my cookie, and it's amazing. Hunger builds, and I realize I can't remember the last time that I ate anything. This cookie is like flipping a switch, as now I'm ravenous.

"I am curious about something," says Oren. "Why did you come back?"

I can't lie to him. Brian's and Justin's deaths might not be my fault, but I still think that Oren deserves the truth.

"Eli told me he'd kill again if I don't."

The door to the coffee shop opens, and I jump. It's a stranger, though.

"Have you told this to the police?" asks Oren.

"Not yet."

"Why?"

"I thought they'd do something to stop me."

He thinks this over. "They probably would. Have you thought about letting them? Stop you, I mean."

I shake my head. "I can't."

"Why not?"

"If I do what he asks, then I'm buying time before anyone

else gets hurt. But you're right, I should tell the cops. I will after this."

"What if you just leave? Don't get me wrong, I'm liking getting to know you, but you might be safer somewhere else."

"He'd keep killing until I come back, I know that. And I won't be able to live with myself if I did nothing and someone else paid for it."

He chews his lip. "I want you to be safe."

"Me too."

He sips his coffee. "In that case, can I help?"

"How?"

"If he asks you to do anything, tell me and I'll come with you."

"It'll be dangerous."

"He killed my friends, Sam. Right now I don't want anything other than to get him behind bars."

"You're sure?"

"I am," he says, and his tone is steady. I don't think he's lying to me.

"Okay, then."

For the first time, I feel a little flicker of hope. Eli won't be expecting me to team up with someone else to take him down. This gives me an advantage.

Game on.

Chapter Eighteen

Drew Lee goes swimming every day.

It's his routine, and even with everything going on, he needs it. In fact, he thinks he especially needs it right now, after his breakup with June, and what has been going on on campus. He needs to zone out for a while, and to let his mind be numbed by exercise until everything feels less sharp.

He walks through the door to the Munroe pool and looks out. There's one other person in the pool right now, swimming laps. Drew grips the handle of his bag tighter. On a regular day, a sight like this would be a dream come true, because he despises having to share a lane with another person.

Right now he wishes there were more people here.

But it's fine. It's midafternoon, and the dean has said that the campus is safe. He knows he is going to be fine. He always is.

He was a high achiever in high school: top of his class in two subjects and second in a third. He was on the debate team, and all the teachers loved him. He had a girlfriend and was popular. He had everything that society said he should want. But it wasn't enough for him, and he knew it, and now he's here.

Nobody back home really understood why he wanted to leave his home state of Oregon to travel to Santa Cruz. Maybe people would've gotten it if he was going to an Ivy—he had the grades, but none of them felt right. But Munroe did. He couldn't explain it, but getting away from his old life was clearly the right move. It made everything more difficult, and he is sad that his decision to move ended his relationship with June, but he still knows he made the right call. This is where he is meant to be.

His heart aches. *June.* She used to swim with him sometimes. He can't blame her for the breakup—he's the one who decided to leave. Sometimes he thinks he should've tried harder. His parents didn't teach him to be a quitter, and yet he gave up on a relationship that once meant everything to him. But sometimes quitting is the right decision, and things were never going to work out with June, not when he was feeling like this. The simple truth is that he loved her, but he couldn't stay there, and she wouldn't move away from her family, so they never stood a chance.

His family probably is the reason. They were always breathing down his neck, telling him what to do. It's not their life, though. It's his.

He goes into the men's locker room, which is empty. The air is cool, and the whole place is quiet.

"Hello?" he calls. His voice echoes slightly.

He frowns and makes his way to the shower area. There is a row of showers and then three toilet cubicles. One is open, and the others are closed but unlocked. He goes up to the first one and knocks on the door. Nothing.

He pushes it open. Empty.

He goes to the next. He wonders what he would do if the killer was here. Would he have enough time to escape before the killer caught him and cut his guts out?

With the tip of his foot, he pushes the door open. It swings open too hard and bangs into the cubicle wall, making a loud noise. Drew flinches, but the stall is empty.

Phew, he thinks.

He goes back to the lockers and starts to change. Once he's in his Speedo, he goes through to the showers and turns on the tap. A steady spray of water comes out, and he steps under it, wetting his hair. He turns around to make sure he has eyes on the entrance.

Brian and Justin are both dead. The killer is still out there. He needs to be careful.

He turns off the water, then goes back out to the pool. The water stretches before him, still and pristine. He dips his goggles into the water and then puts them on.

He knows that, soon, the exercise will make his mind shut up. If he pushes himself hard enough, that is.

He dives into the water, barely making a ripple as he breaks the surface. He swims underwater for as long as he can, until he comes up for air and starts swimming toward the end at full speed.

June. Brian. Justin.

He reaches the end of the pool, then flips under, and then pushes off. He turns his head, to take in a breath. He swims up, and back, up and back, as if he is in a trance. Drew has never meditated, but he thinks that swimming works the same way for him. It's one of the few times he feels peace. The other person swimming gets out of the pool and leaves, but he keeps going. He's in the zone now.

He swims up, and back, until his whole body starts to burn.

Drew turns his head and notices someone is by the pool, and he stops swimming. He gapes at the figure standing poolside, holding a knife. The Freak turns his head.

"Hello, Drew."

Drew spins, and starts swimming to the other side of the pool as fast as he can. The Freak runs, trying to cut him off. Drew climbs out of the pool and just manages to stand upright before the Freak reaches him and slashes down with his knife, cutting Drew on the back. A diagonal line of red appears, and Drew's blood starts to mix with the pool water on his back. Drew lets out a cry, turns back, and wildly punches the Freak hard enough to knock him to the ground. Drew sees his chance and runs for the exit. He reaches it and tries the door, but it's locked.

"Help!" he shouts. He smacks his hand on the glass door, leaving a bloody handprint.

In view, the security guard is on the floor in a pool of blood. His throat has been slashed.

Drew turns, just in time to see the Freak reach him and swing with his knife. Drew ducks under and runs for the locker room, and his phone.

He skids into the room and grabs his bag from the locker. His phone falls out and bounces once on the ground before landing facedown. He reaches for it, but the Freak kicks him, knocking him over. Drew flips around as the killer advances, his knife raised.

"Fuck you," spits Drew.

The Freak stops.

Drew sees his chance and kicks at the Freak's crotch as hard as he can. The Freak buckles, and Drew gets up and grabs his phone and runs into the shower area. He goes into a toilet stall and locks it, then perches on the toilet, so his feet aren't exposed. His phone screen is covered in a spiderweb of cracks, and his bloody hands make dialing difficult, but he still manages to call 911.

"911. What is your emergency?"

"I'm being attacked—send someone, please!"

"What's your location?"

Drew pauses for a moment, then takes a breath. "I'm in the pool at Munroe University."

The Freak bangs against the cubicle door.

"He's here," says Drew. "Hurry."

"Calm down; who is there?"

"The killer!"

"Hold tight, police officers are outside; they'll be there in a second."

The Freak reaches under the cubicle and swipes with his knife but misses. He starts banging his shoulder against the door as hard as he can. Drew hisses with pain as he turns his head around to try to see his wound. All he sees is the blood coating his back. There's so much of it that he starts getting light-headed. He leans his head against the wall.

There's another bang against the door, and then silence.

Drew waits. Is he gone, or is this a trick?

A few moments later, footsteps sound outside.

"Son?"

It's a new voice, but Drew doesn't want to open the door. This could be a trick of the killer's.

"I'm on your side, it's okay."

"It's okay," says a different voice, a woman's. "You're safe, he's gone."

Drew gets up and uses his last reserve of energy to open the door. He falls out of the cubicle, landing at the feet of two police officers.

I did it, he thinks. *I'm safe.*

Chapter Nineteen

It's happened again.

I'm outside the pool building, among a crowd of people who have come to watch. I feel eyes on me and spot Alyson watching me. In the crowd are a bunch of brothers and pledges, including Tripp, Mikey, Booker, and Oren, watching crestfallen as Drew is wheeled out of the pool building by a paramedic. The security guard wasn't so lucky. I don't know his name, but that makes three dead now.

Drew is sitting up, and his torso is wrapped in bandages. It's a miracle that he's still alive. I want to say that it must've been Drew's quick thinking that saved him, but that would be unfair to Justin and Brian. I'm sure they were just as smart and capable, but for some reason Drew managed to survive when they didn't.

Beside Tripp, Beth lets out a loud sob. He puts his arm around her, and she nestles into him. There's something about it that seems a little faked. Like, on her podcast she explicitly says that she loves murder. How can she go from that to suddenly weeping? I know it's different when it's happening to people you know, and yet . . .

There's something about it that seems off.

I'm not sure why I am considering her a suspect. I know who did this. He might be wearing a mask, but we have the footage of him taking it off. It is Eli. He is doing this. But that still doesn't feel right to me. I don't know how the sweet, sensitive boy I knew could turn into a killer. People can change a lot in two years, I am a testament to that, but I think there are changes that are within the realm of possibility, and then there's Eli turning into a cold-blooded killer hell-bent on revenge.

I don't even know why I'm considering it isn't Eli. It's wishful thinking, probably. Now isn't the time for that. Now is the time for action, and that means I need to stall Eli. I write him a message and hit send.

I've done everything you asked. Why did you attack Drew?

Across the crowd, Beth gets a notification on her phone. She stares at it and starts typing.

I'm starting to feel a little like Charlie Day from that conspiracy theory meme. I can't help it.

The story as it stands doesn't line up. Why would Eli be killing all these people?

Every time I decide that it's impossible, I get slammed with the cold, hard truth. He is. They have camera footage of him. And unless it was somehow faked by the police, then it has to be him.

But why?

I haven't had enough time to really explore that yet, but now I'm becoming slightly fixated on it. What's Eli's motive? We did break up, but that was amicable. We fell out of each other's lives, but that happens after breakups, and couples who date in high school often don't end up together forever. It doesn't mean that someone would go from a sweetheart to a mask-wearing killer. Even if Eli was acting when we split up, and he secretly wanted to be together, which feels like a reach, I don't think that is enough of a motive to kill three people and to try to kill another to make me suffer.

The other option that I can think of is that the lake house broke him. That one is maybe a little more plausible, but still doesn't exactly feel right. The Freak's actions seem too pointed for that. He wants to make me suffer as much as he can.

My phone vibrates. It's from Eli.

Did I tell you you could tell the cops about this? If you break the rules, somebody will pay, Sam.

He's getting desperate, probably because he knows it can't be too much longer before the cops find him. I need to stay focused and not let this get under my skin. My goal is to keep him playing this game for as long as I can, because as long as he's focused on tormenting me, he's not killing anyone.

I'm sorry. I'll do whatever you want from now on.

I know you will.

"Who are you texting?"

I lower my phone and find Mikey staring me down.

"I asked you a question," says Mikey as he points a finger in my face. His cheeks are flushed, and I can see a vein throbbing in his neck.

"My dad," I say.

"You're lying."

He shoves me in the chest, and I stagger back. The crowd around us parts and starts staring.

"You did this!" he shouts. "It's you!"

"I didn't."

"Okay, where were you?"

"That's none of your fucking business."

"That's not an answer. Everyone's saying it, Sam. It's you."

"Fuck you, Mikey."

I see his hand move, and lightning-fast something smacks into my cheek, and then I feel myself collapsing. He just punched me in the face. He's looking down at me now, his chest heaving. That fucking fucker. I clench my fist. He can't punch me and expect to get away with it. There's no way.

I spring up, but a body comes out of nowhere, blocking

me. Oren. I try to push past him, but he grabs my arms, forcing me to meet his stare.

"He's not worth it," he says.

"Break it up!" shouts a voice. I turn and see Fukuda and McDougall making their way to us.

"You're coming with us," says McDougall, and he roughly turns Mikey around to handcuff him.

"Arrest him!" shouts Mikey as the cuffs click on around his wrists. I won't lie, it's a satisfying sight. "He's the killer!"

Fukuda comes up to me. "Are you okay?"

I touch my cheek and wince. I pull my fingers back and find a small amount of blood on my fingertips.

"I'm fine," I say.

"You should go to the hospital," says Oren. "I can take you."

"I'm okay."

The truth is I hate hospitals. I hate the way they smell. Just the thought of having to go to one makes my skin crawl.

"Someone should watch him," Fukuda says. "Just for a few hours."

"I can," says Oren. "He can crash with me." He turns to me. "If you want to?"

"Here," says Oren.

He hands me a bag of frozen peas. I take them and press them against my cheek. It stings, and I let out an involuntary hiss of pain. Oren has taken me back to his room, and I'm sitting on his couch.

"How does it feel?" asks Oren.

"Sore."

"Do you want a Tylenol?"

"Yes, please."

He goes over to his closet and rummages around until he finds a first aid kit. He brings it back and sits down beside me.

"I'm sorry about Mikey," he says. "Are you going to press charges?"

I shake my head. A part of me wants to, but as rude as he has been to me, I know he is lashing out because of fear. And I don't want to ruin his life. It was just a hit; I'll be fine.

"I doubt he's going to be a brother much longer, if hearing that helps at all."

"It doesn't," I say as he hands me a packet of Tylenol. "It's not his fault."

"I think it is."

"He's scared; it's okay."

"I don't know if I could be so chill," he says.

"I try my best."

He gets me a glass of water, and I swallow the pills.

Hopefully it works, because a pretty major headache is starting to come on.

"He wasn't always like that," he says. "He used to be different."

"I assumed, I mean, I can't picture you dating someone like him."

"I get you. I think he's a good guy, deep down. But very self-centered."

"Is that why you broke up?"

He looks down.

"Sorry," I say. "I shouldn't have asked that."

"It's fine. I had something really bad happen last year, and Mikey wasn't equipped to deal with what I was going through."

"I'm sorry, that was shit of him."

"Yeah, it was. If you can forgive him for hitting you, I should probably forgive him for not wanting to deal with my grief."

Wait, grief? Oren lost someone?

"I'm sorry, I didn't know," I say.

"It's okay, I don't really talk about it. I'll tell you about it sometime, all right?"

"Okay, whenever you're ready."

Chapter Twenty

I wince as the doctor touches my wound.

I'm sitting in an examination room. I didn't want to come here, and I actually only did because of Drew. It's been a few hours since he was attacked, and the doctors finally said he could have visitors, and all of the pledge class has decided to come here in order to show our support. If it weren't for that, there's no way I'd be here. Oren convinced me that if I was here anyway, I may as well see a doctor, and I couldn't argue with that.

Still, I hate it here. Everything about this place reeks of death.

"It's not going to need stitches," she says. "But it's important to keep it clean—you don't want it getting infected." She covers the cut with a gauze dressing, which hits me with a fresh wave of pain. "How's your head feeling?"

"Sore, but it's getting better."

"That's good. And you're sure you didn't hit your head when you fell?"

"Yeah, I didn't."

"Good. It'll take you a few days for the cut to heal, and you'll have some bruising, but you'll be okay."

"Glad to hear it."

"Keep an eye out for any changes. If you feel light-headed at all, or your headache gets worse, come back here. Head injuries can be tricky."

She guides me over to the door and opens it for me.

"Thanks," I say.

"You're very welcome."

I go outside and find myself in a long hospital hallway. I go down and then around a corner to where the pledge class has assembled, along with a few of the brothers and McDougall. Oren is sitting by himself with a pair of earbuds in. I go up to him, and he takes his earbuds out and puts them back in their case.

"What'd they say?" he asks.

"I'll be fine. I just need to keep it clean."

"Cool."

Booker leaves Drew's room and notices me. He makes his way across.

"Drew said he'd like to see you," he says.

I get up and go into Drew's room. He's sitting up in a hospital bed, wearing a light blue gown. A drip is attached to his arm, and his skin is pale, but he looks pretty okay, considering. He got so lucky.

"Can you close the door?" he asks.

"Sure."

I close it and then go up to him. What should I say to him? Everything seems too superficial, not reflective of the gravity of the situation. I can't outright apologize for what Eli did.

"I heard about Mikey," he says. "Are you all right?"

"I should be asking you that."

He smiles, then his face contorts with pain. "It's not a deep cut; I'll be out by tomorrow."

"That's good."

"Yeah. But back to Mikey. I also heard what he said, and, dude, I want you to know I don't blame you."

I grip the railing of his bed. I have been making progress on not blaming myself for what has been going on, because even if I am a part of it, I am an unwilling participant, and Eli is the one to blame for it all. And yet, hearing Drew say those words lifts a huge weight from me, making it so I can finally breathe again.

"Thank you," I say.

"We're brothers," he says, offering me a fist bump.

I touch my knuckles against his, careful not to push too hard.

"We're in this together."

Chapter Twenty-One

Get dressed and go down to the Munroe statue on the quad. If you're not there in five minutes, I'll kill. Tell the pigs if you want, it won't change anything.

I grab a shirt from my closet and put it on. Then I pull a pair of jeans over my boxers and put on my shoes. I've been home from the hospital for only a few hours, and I spent that time trying, and failing, to catch up on sleep. Once I'm dressed and ready, I grab my Taser, then leave the room. In the hallway, I call Fukuda. She picks up on the second ring.

"Sam?"

I jam the elevator door button. "Eli messaged me."

"What did he say?"

"He wants me to go to the Munroe statue on campus. He's going to be there."

"I'm on my way."

I hang up as the elevator doors finally open. I get a message from Eli.

Three minutes.

I type out a text to Oren, and once it's done, I delete it.

If Eli is out there, I don't want Oren there, too. I can't risk anything happening to him.

The moon is about half full, and the air is brisk enough that the hairs on my arms and on the back of my neck rise. I increase my pace to a near sprint and try to stop myself from looking down the alleyways. There's no point. Eli won't do anything, not yet. This is just part of the game. He must be expecting me to call the cops, so he must have a contingency for that—it doesn't matter.

Still, this can end tonight if the police can catch him.

I reach the Munroe statue and skid to a stop. I'm here.

But I'm a minute too slow.

There is a box sitting in front of the statue. My phone starts to ring, making me jump.

I swipe and accept the call.

"Hello?"

"Hello, Sam."

I turn around, trying to find him. I can't see him. He must be here, somewhere.

"You were too slow," he says.

"Eli, please . . ."

"Open the box."

I go up to it. It seems fairly innocent, just a regular cardboard box, but there must be something horrific in there if Eli is forcing me to open it. I just have to hope it's only more doll heads. I lift open the lid and recoil instantly. I only saw a flash of it, but it was enough for me to know what it is.

It's Justin's severed head.

My stomach twists, and I bend over. I try to stop it, but I can't, and I throw up.

He made me come out here to see this. In the distance, I see flashing red and blue lights. I wipe my mouth as a police station wagon pulls up in front of me. Fukuda climbs out and takes her gun out of her holster, holding it at the ready.

"What happened?" she asks.

"It's Justin" is all I manage to say.

I glance at the box, and she figures it out, and brings her hands up to her mouth.

Chapter Twenty-Two

Tripp always works out at night.

It's the only time the gym isn't filled with skinny, annoying people who don't know what they're doing. It's infuriating watching them be so totally useless. They don't know the correct form, and they never focus on progressive overload. Out of the gym, they probably don't eat enough protein, which makes what they're doing in here almost totally useless. Plus, they hog all the machines, so he has to wait.

He hates waiting.

The best solution he's found to avoid the problem with annoying gym goers is to go late at night. He's just walked into the campus gym now, scanning his pass on the glass door outside, and finds himself with a dream sight: a completely empty gym. He knows he probably shouldn't be here, but he can't risk losing his gains.

Tripp goes over to the screen on the wall and picks "Without Me" by Eminem. Seeing as there's nobody else here, there are no songs lined up, and it starts playing immediately through the speakers spaced out around the gym. Tripp's lips tug up into a crooked smile.

He grabs a big set of dumbbells, bigger than most of his brothers can lift, and starts doing curls.

One. Two. Three.

Once he's done, he drops the weights. Nothing beats this. He's stronger than he was last time. It means his program is working. He's learned that the scales can't be trusted, and it's been a while since he's noticed an obvious big visual change in his size. It's difficult to build on perfection. The best way to track his strength is the weights themselves, and the proof is in the pudding, as his dad says.

He does another set, then drops the weights again. He grabs his phone and frowns at the screen. No new messages. What is Beth's problem? She left him on read when he asked if she would like to watch a movie tonight—not that he'd expect them to make it past the Netflix selection screen.

He does one more set, racks the weights, and starts doing push-ups. He has a plan now, and he could have the best pump after his workout, but he doesn't have the patience for that.

He lifts his tank top over his head and tosses it away. His body is a work of art, every muscle defined. He pulls his gym shorts down a little, not to show anything too sexual save for the deep Adonis lines that took years to come in, then pulls a serious face and starts taking selfies. Once he's done, he checks them, and they are good, but they're missing something. He goes back to the locker and grabs his baseball cap. He puts it on backward, then gets back into position and tries again.

This time, when he checks the pictures, he's happy. He sends one to Beth. And one to Amber for good measure.

Now he waits.

He goes over to the bench press bar and starts loading it with weights. The gym has a rule that shirts need to stay on, but he doubts he's going to get in trouble this late in an empty gym. He's also supposed to use a gym towel, but fuck that. He's clean, it's fine.

He then lies down, not bothering to put on the safety bars. He knows what he's doing.

He lowers the bar, grunts, and pushes up. His arms tremble.

His pecs and arms are burning now, but he relishes the pain. It means it's working, and he'll get bigger and stronger.

Once he's finished his reps, he sits up and grabs his phone.

Both girls have responded with pictures.

Beth is in a gray hoodie on the couch, holding up a block of white chocolate, her favorite. He has never met anyone who likes white chocolate as much as her. Or anyone who likes white chocolate period, to be honest. Amber has sent back a picture of her own. She's in a red bra and is biting her bottom lip. He knows which one he is seeing tonight.

He really likes Beth. She's great, and he likes dating her. But Amber . . . what guy could resist a girl like that?

He returns his attention to the weights. He won't respond for a while, anyway. It's all part of his strategy, and it always works. Girls like a little mystery. He will respond, but he may as well let them sweat it out for a little. He knows he always appreciates it when girls mess with his head a little; it makes their eventual time together so much more fun. Maybe that's why he likes Amber so much. She's unpredictable.

Tripp lies down and unhooks the bar. Now that his arms are sore, it's much harder. He lowers the bar to his chest, but when he tries to push up, his arms fail him.

Out of the corner of his eye, he notices someone coming up to him.

"Bro," says Tripp. "Can you give me a spot?"

The person jumps up, landing on Tripp's chest. Tripp drops the bar, and it lands on his neck. Tripp recognizes the person perched on top of him: He's the killer. The Freak presses the bar down onto Tripp's neck. The boy flails, trying to knock the masked figure off him, or to get the bar off his neck, but he can't.

He chokes and wraps his fingers around the bar, trying to push it up and off, but he's not strong enough.

The Freak pulls a knife from his back pocket and raises it up. Tripp tries to scream, but he can't.

The Freak stabs down, cutting into Tripp's chest. He pulls the knife out and stabs again.

Tripp's arms go slack, and they drop off the bar.

He tries to fight back the darkness, but he's not strong enough.

Chapter Twenty-Three

Hey, are you free?

It's from Oren, and I'm not sure I have the energy to respond.

Tripp was murdered last night. They found his body in the gym this morning. Despite my efforts, and those of the cops, we weren't enough. And now Tripp is dead, too. It's too much for me. So yes. In answer to his question, I am free. It's just that there's a difference between being free and having enough energy to do something with him.

Clearly, Eli is killing people who are close to me. And if I spend time with Oren, then I am making him a target.

Yeah, what's up?

Nothing, I was wondering if you would like to come to the boxing gym with me?

You box?

I don't fight anyone, but I like learning the technique. I am also noticing that you haven't said no. There are cops everywhere on campus now btw, we'll be safe.

You sure you're okay with it?

I wouldn't have offered if I wasn't. We'll be safe.

This morning all I've been doing is wallowing in my room, fighting the urge to be sick. This doesn't help anyone. What I need to do is figure out a way to catch Eli, and clearly staying in my room isn't getting me any closer to achieving that. At all. Maybe a change of scenery will get my mind working enough to figure out a way to trap Eli. In order to beat him, I need to be a step ahead of him. That is impossible right now, given I don't understand why he is doing what he is.

I can meet you there in half an hour?

Looking forward to it.

I rub my temples. How am I supposed to get a step ahead of him if I don't understand who he is anymore?

I load the details into my Maps app and then look down at my shirt. I'm wearing an old gray tee. I change into my best workout outfit, and then in the mirror I start preening my hair. I always used to, but with everything going on it seems the least of my worries. Then I realize what I'm doing—or, more important, why I'm doing it, so I tousle my hair, messing it up again. I grab my Taser, pocket it, then I leave my room.

It's another perfect day outside. Oren was right, the campus is crawling with police. *Good*. A pair of girls walking by gawk at me, but I ignore them. I would wear a hoodie and keep the hood up, but that would limit my field of vision, and

I don't want to take any big risks like that. I've practiced it countless times, so I know that I can get my Taser out of my pocket quickly if I need to. If Eli rushes me, I can stop him.

A small part of me hopes he does attack me now. I have my Taser. If he attacks, maybe this can all end, and things can get back to normal and nobody else innocent will get hurt.

As I walk, I think about the life that has been denied to me by Eli. I guess that's his motivation, if only because nothing else makes any sense: I was so close to having a life I enjoyed that didn't include him. *So* close. Maybe he knew that and didn't want me to have that life without him. This makes some sense to me, but at the same time, I can't believe that the boy who cried at the end of *Encanto* is capable of murder just to hurt me. I picture Eli kneeling over Brian's body, using a knife to carve my name into his flesh, or cutting off Justin's head to freak me out. It still seems wrong, like it can't be him, even though I know that it is.

It's him. Trying to deny that doesn't help anyone.

I reach the boxing gym and go inside. Oren's already working out in the corner. I go up to him, and he pauses his workout, using his hand to stop the swinging punching bag. His chest is heaving, and sweat has made it so his tank clings to him, showing off the very pleasing definition of his chest.

"Ready?" he asks.

"Yep."

It's a wide room, with brick walls and a boxing ring in the middle. A small handful of other students are working out around the place, but nobody is using the ring. One person stands out: a bald, muscular guy who must be nearing forty, so he'd be close to double the age of everyone else here. Maybe he's a teacher, or a cop in disguise. At the back of the room the word *Patriots* is painted on the brick in huge letters, from floor to ceiling.

"Have you done this before?" he asks.

"Nope. I have my own way of defending myself."

I take out my Taser and show him.

"That'll work," he says.

I have thought about taking some self-defense classes. I haven't wanted to because in a way, that felt like acknowledging one of my deepest fears: that I would find myself in that situation again. Why learn how to defend yourself unless you expect that? Plus, training might help a small amount, but I'm worried it would make me overconfident. Even with a Taser, if someone attacks you with a knife or a gun, the best strategy is to put as much distance between you and them as possible.

"What do I do?" I ask as I get in front of the punching bag. "Just hit it?"

"Go ahead."

I punch the bag lightly.

Oren crosses his arms. "Harder."

I punch again, properly this time.

"Feels good, right?" he asks.

I smile. Because yeah, it really does feel good. I punch again. It hurts my knuckles a little, but it's totally a release. It feels better than good. It feels *amazing*.

"Can I give you some advice?" he asks.

I hit the bag again. "Yep."

"Bend your knees a little. Then turn."

He demonstrates, dropping his back leg a little before striking. I get into position and then punch the bag again. The difference is night and day. Even with less effort, the punch had way more power.

"He's a natural," says Oren.

I smile and punch the bag again. And again. I totally get why people do this: It makes me feel strong and powerful. I would never want to fight someone, but maybe I could start boxing classes, if only to chase this feeling.

I move aside, letting him have a go at the bag. His face sets in concentration, and he punches the bag so hard it swings. He pulls his fist back, and it's clear his movements are heavily practiced. He punches again, and it's just as perfect. It's pretty freaking hot. He obviously does this a lot, and it feels unfair that I don't know this pretty big part of him, simply because I haven't asked.

"I'm sorry," I say.

He stops. "For what?"

"I feel like I haven't asked you much about yourself. I didn't even know you boxed."

"That's totally understandable, Sam."

"I know, I just want you to know you can tell me stuff about you. If you want."

"Are you asking me out, Carville?"

I start to blush, and I'm so self-conscious that he can see. I didn't think I was, and yet the thought doesn't freak me out. It feels warm, and comfortable. Oren has been nothing but sweet with me, and he is incredibly cute. If I got to go out with him, I would feel incredibly lucky.

"I . . . Er . . ."

"I mean, I would like to go out with you," he says. "As soon as this is all over."

Wait, did I hear that correctly? Oren kind of asked me out on a date? I remember that I need to respond.

"Um, yeah. When this is all over. Definitely."

It's hard to picture, given everything. But I do know this with total clarity: I'd like that. I'd like to sit opposite Oren as we got dinner, and he could tell me about his life. I'd like that a lot, actually.

"Can't wait," he says.

Chapter Twenty-Four

Go to the Soho motel tonight at 7 p.m. Stay there until I say you can leave.

That's in half an hour.

Why would Eli want me to do this? On my phone, I look up the Soho, and find that it's an old motel on the outskirts of town. Maybe that's where he's staying? Although if that were the case, surely the police would've found him by now. Eli may have been able to slip through the cops' fingers so far, but I don't think that's because they're incompetent. I think it's because Eli is a few steps ahead of them, and has probably spent a long time planning out what he is going to do.

This is the next part of his game. Getting me to go to the Soho for reasons unknown.

I message Fukuda and then Oren.

Oren responds first.

I'm coming with you. I'll grab my car and pick you up in five minutes? Stay in your room until I message you.

I don't feel great about it, but I don't really have a choice.

I don't have a car, and while I could take a Lyft or something, that means I would have to spend the night at a rundown motel with Eli still on the loose. If I have to do this, I would much prefer to spend the night in a car.

A call comes in from Fukuda.

"What do you think he's planning?" she asks.

"I'm not sure. But you'll be there, right?"

"I will. I'll be in plain clothes. Do you have a car?"

"Yeah, I'm going with my friend Oren."

"Perfect. Stay in your car, don't get out for anything, all right? If he tries something, I'll catch him."

Perfect.

All right. I have a plan, but this still feels terrifying. The last time Eli asked me to go somewhere, he wanted to show me a severed head, and something is telling me that whatever he wants to show me tonight is going to be worse. I have no idea what could be worse than seeing a severed head, but I'm sure Eli has something in mind.

He must truly hate me. Like, deeply. This whole thing is clearly totally planned, and that sort of thing takes time. He had the time to make the Freak's mask. Wait.

I haven't really thought about this before, but why would Eli wear the Freak's mask? There's no real reason for him to do that. If he wanted to traumatize me, why wouldn't he wear a balaclava, like Shawn did?

No.

I'm doing it again, and I can't. Even if my gut is telling me that Eli can't be the Freak, because it doesn't line up, there is still that security camera footage. It's him. There's no point exploring other theories when that photo exists.

My phone vibrates, making me jump.

I'm here.

Here it goes, I guess.

Outside, Oren is waiting in the driver's seat of a sleek black car. I'm not really a car guy, because driving made me anxious even before the lake, but there's no mistaking that this is a very nice car. It must've been a gift from his parents, because Oren doesn't seem to have a day job, and even then, a journalism student with a part-time job wouldn't have the amount of money to afford such a nice vehicle. I get inside, and the interior is just as nice, with soft tan leather seats, spotlessly clean.

Oren taps on the screen on the dash.

"It's the Soho, right?" he asks.

"Yep."

He enters the details, and I see it'll be a five-minute drive. We have plenty of time, and Eli isn't going to be able to use lateness as an excuse to kill again. Oren turns down the radio, quieting "A Dustland Fairytale" by the Killers.

"I love this song," he says.

"Me too."

"Really?"

"My dad loves the Killers; they're one of his favorite bands."

"He has good taste."

"I wouldn't go that far."

Oren chuckles.

The rest of the drive passes quickly, and all too soon, we're pulling up at the front of the Soho motel with a few minutes to spare. It's a low building with a big yellow-and-red sign out front. There are only a few crappy cars parked in the lot. In one of them is Fukuda, in plain clothes. I'm not so sure that this was a good idea. It's starting to get hot, and sweat is already forming on the back of my neck.

Above the parking lot is a big purple neon sign saying VACANCY. I doubt that's ever been a problem; I would be shocked if this place was ever completely booked. This is the sort of motel that people want to stay in when they're getting away from something, or maybe doing something they don't want anyone in the real world to know about. Because that's the feeling of the place: It's an actual liminal space. It's somehow detached from normal reality.

"What now?" asks Oren as he taps his fingers against the leather of the steering wheel.

"We wait, I guess."

He leans back in his seat. "I've never been good at that. If something is going to happen, I want it to happen, you know?"

"Same."

Oren peers out the front window. "Someone's out there."

He's right. A balding man in an ill-fitting suit has just emerged from a room on the upper level. His stare is shifty, and he looks around, clearly hoping that nobody has seen him. Is he who Eli wants us to see? There's seemingly nothing out of the ordinary about the man, even if his body language is giving off the impression that he has done something that he is ashamed of.

"Do you recognize him?" I ask.

"Nope."

The man goes down the steps, then gets into his car. He swings around in front of us and turns, catching both Oren and me looking at him. He stares back with wide eyes and raised eyebrows before he passes.

"Want to bet who is in there?" asks Oren. "Drug dealer or affair?"

I think it over.

"Affair," I say.

"See, I'm going to bet it's drugs. I'll bet you ten dollars I'm right."

"I'll take that bet."

It takes about ten minutes for the door to open, and a woman emerges from the room. I start smiling.

"Um," says Oren. "You don't know she isn't a dealer."

The woman gets into her car and drives away. The

motel goes still. I doubt that's what Eli wanted me to see. That man might be messing up his life, but I don't know what that would have to do with the murders going on at Munroe.

Oren's phone buzzes. It's on the dash, facedown.

"I don't want to check it," he says. "It's always bad news lately."

"I know."

Eli shouldn't have attacked someone else tonight. He wanted us here for a reason. It wouldn't make much sense for him to send us here and not witness whatever it is that he wants us to see.

Oren checks his phone, then reads the message. His expression doesn't change.

"Who was it?"

"Nothing, just spam."

He shoves his phone into his pocket. Okay. That was weird. If it was spam, why didn't he just show me? It's definitely unfair of me to be suspicious of Oren after everything he has done to help me. And yet, if it was spam, why didn't he look relieved when he saw it? It's almost as if he tried to keep his reaction from being visible. There are only two reasons he would do that: If someone else was hurt and he doesn't want me to know about it, or he is up to something.

He takes his phone out of his pocket, unlocks it, and shows me the screen.

It's a text message from Domino's, offering him a two-for-one deal on their value range of pizzas.

"Sorry," I say.

"You don't have to be sorry. I understand."

"It's hard for me to trust people. But I do trust you."

"I trust you, too." He stares out the window. "I've been thinking, and I would like to tell you what happened last year, if you want to hear it?"

"I do."

Tears well in his eyes. "Sorry. It's still really hard to say."

I shift in my seat so I'm facing him more. Whatever Eli has planned for me can wait for a few moments, because Oren is going to open up to me. Obviously this is very hard for him to say, as his whole body is shaking.

"My brother, Harrison . . . he died last year," he says. "He was my best friend."

It makes things come into focus. Things between Mikey and Oren ended because Mikey couldn't handle Oren's grief. But he lost a brother. I have no idea how devastating that must be for Oren, to have a man he loved bail on him when he probably needed him the most. And seriously, what is Mikey's problem? Oren lost his brother, that's not something you just get over. If anything happened to Gus I would never get over it.

"It was cancer," continues Oren, who is still on the verge of tears. He breathes in deep, then exhales. "He had it when he was younger, but then it came back. It was so fast."

"I'm so sorry."

"He'd be so upset with me if he knew how depressed I've been. He was a ball of energy. He'd want me to live my life, but it's so hard without him."

"I know."

"I just wish I had him back. He was only ten, Sam."

He scrubs a hand across his eyes. We go silent for a while. Sometimes words can't help. Not with things like this.

After a while, Oren turns to me. "You really impressed me when you came here."

"In what way?"

"I've been trying to hide what happened. I didn't think people would like me if they knew how messed up my past is. You didn't hide it. I don't want what happened to Harrison to define me, but I don't want to keep hiding it."

"I get you."

"And you aren't, Sam. You aren't defined by what happened to you."

"I sometimes feel like I am."

"You're not."

He was honest with me, and I want to be honest with him. I don't want to hold anything back. Not anymore.

"I used to want to be a writer," I say. "But after the lake, I stopped."

"Why?"

"If everyone knew what I'd done, would anyone want to read a book by me?"

"Sam, yes. You're more than what happened to you. I know I've only just met you, but I feel . . ."

My heart catches. "What?"

"Something, I guess."

I understand him, because I am right there with him. *Something*. Such a casual word, and yet, it's massive. Because for the longest time I didn't think that I would be able to feel anything else for someone. Not even a crush, or passing interest. That part of me was completely dead. And yet, just setting my eyes on Oren is enough to make me feel it. It might not be a crush yet, but it's certainly a flicker, and who knows what it could grow into. Where there was once nothing, there is now something.

"Me too," I say.

Between us, my phone buzzes.

It's from Eli.

Go to room 201. You have two minutes.

I show Oren the message.

"She said not to leave the car," Oren says.

"I don't have a choice."

I get out and fold my arms across my chest to try to hide my trembling arms. Eli will be here somewhere, and I don't want to give him the satisfaction of seeing me scared. I scan the golden numbers on the motel room doors, counting down to room 201. Rotting leaves are spread across the empty parking lot, and the building could desperately use a fresh coat of paint: The yellow walls have faded so much they're almost white.

I take out my Taser as Oren climbs out of his car. We cross the lot and go up the stairs, then down the walkway until we reach the door.

"Sam!"

It's Fukuda; she's chased us up the stairs.

"What are you doing?" she asks.

"Eli told me to come here."

She glances at the door. "Why?"

"I don't know."

My phone goes off.

Knock.

"He wants me to knock," I say.

"You sure about this?" asks Oren.

I rap my fist against the door and pull my hand back. Fukuda unholsters her gun and holds it at the ready.

The door unlocks and then opens. I gape for a moment, because this can't be happening.

Standing in front of me is my mom.

Chapter Twenty-Five

"Sam," she says. "What are you doing here?"

It's pretty freaking obvious that she wasn't expecting me to see her, and it's also pretty freaking obvious why she is here. She's a stuck writer who hasn't been able to finish a book since she ripped off the worst night of my life. She's here to mine my life for story ideas once again.

She's going to write a fucking sequel.

"I'll give you some space," says Fukuda, and she backs away.

I turn back to Mom.

"What are you doing here?" I say.

I don't want to shout at her. Or I do and don't at the same time. Even if she has just shown herself to be one of the most selfish people on the planet, she's still my mom. I don't want to yell at her. What I want is for her to be miles away from here. I feel someone watching me and see Fukuda standing by her station wagon. She climbs inside and closes the door.

Mom glances warily to the side, to Oren. He has his

arms crossed and is looking at my mom with more disdain than I thought he was possible of expressing. He's livid.

"I came to support you," she says. "But I couldn't bring myself to see you."

"You're lying."

"I'm not. I've tried to message you every day . . ."

"You've been here for *days?*"

She starts wringing her hands. Days. She's been here for days. She's probably gone to campus multiple times, being careful to avoid me, but making sure she's as close to the story as possible. I don't understand how someone can act like her. I'm her son. Her child. And she hasn't bothered to call me to try to provide any comfort or assistance. She saw all of this happening on the news and was probably happy, because now she has the basis for her next book. For all I know she's already spoken to her publisher and has a deal to write a sequel.

She steps closer. "I need to be here, Sam. It's my job."

Oren mutters something under his breath.

"Who are you?" asks Mom, turning on him and becoming furious. "You think this is funny, huh?"

Oren juts his chin up.

"You're judging me!" she says. "You don't know me."

"Why are you yelling?" asks Oren. "Don't you see what you've done?"

"I'm not going to be told how to live my life by someone I've never met!"

"You're right," I say. "Let's go."

"Sam, stay. I can explain myself. There's a reason I'm here: My publisher has offered enough money that I can set you and Gus up for life. I could give both of you a solid deposit for a house."

"I don't want that from you, can't you see that? I want you to be a normal mom. You could've just asked me, but you didn't."

"I was going to."

This conversation is going around in circles already, and from past arguments with Mom I know that it isn't going to change. She will snap at me like she snapped at Oren, but she is always convinced that she's right. In her brain, she is doing the right thing, and there is no getting around that. We could fight all night, and her stance won't change at all. She'll just dig herself further into her beliefs.

I can't dignify that with a response, so I turn and start walking back toward the car. I hurry across the lot. Oren unlocks his car before I open the door. I still check the back seat, in case, and it's empty. Oren gets in and closes his door.

I'm totally numb.

It's too much of an overload for me to handle right now.

I've known for a long time that Mom is selfish and only cares about herself and her career, but I guess I had started thinking that she might change after what her decisions did to our family. Her decision to write about me the first time ruined her marriage. She left Gus behind to be raised by Dad and she didn't seem to be bothered by that at all. She hurt all of us so much, and it just doesn't matter to her.

"Where do you want to go?" asks Oren.

I don't know. I don't think it matters. There's nowhere I can go that will change what just happened.

Oren starts to drive. I can't look at him, I'll break down if I do. Oren drives a few blocks, then pulls over and parks. Down the street is a 24/7 diner. Oren turns off the engine, and everything goes silent.

I realize something.

She didn't even apologize. It confirms what I was thinking. She can act like that and still not see anything wrong with her actions. She might be using the small fortune her publisher offered her in order to justify this call. There's no way she didn't think about all the benefits she will get. Continued literary relevance. A healthy sum for herself. More social media followers.

That's what she cares about more than me. And Gus. And Dad.

I can't hold it back, and I start to cry.

"Oh, Sam," says Oren.

"She doesn't care," I say between sobs. I want to stop, because I don't want to cry in front of Oren. I can't help it.

"I'm sorry," says Oren.

"I . . ."

I turn away from Oren and look out at the diner. I'm having such a strong emotional reaction because that is probably the nail in the coffin of my relationship with Mom. She's already broken my heart once—or a few times, really—but this time is different. This time, there's no coming back from it.

I just lost my mom forever.

"What can I do to help?" asks Oren.

"Nothing."

"If you need anything, I'm here."

I start to cry again. I've known Oren only a few days, and he's already shown me more kindness than Mom has in years. That's so messed up. So many people get parents who care about them, and I know I'm lucky to have Dad, who has always gone above and beyond. Maybe I'm being selfish, but I want a mom who cares this much, too.

"I'm sorry," I say.

"Don't be sorry, it's okay. I get it, it's really tough."

I wipe my eyes. That was the most of it out. I don't feel like crying anymore, but I obviously don't feel great.

We sit for a while, with me staring out the window. My emotions settle and start getting less intense, to the point where I can control them.

I turn to Oren. "Are you hungry?"

"Are you?"

"Yeah."

"Want to go to that diner? I've been a few times, it's good."

We get out of the car and walk toward the diner.

There's a big neon sign on the top, and the entire building is drenched in light, from the green of the wineglass—or maybe it's an ice cream sundae—sticking out the front, to the strips of blue and red running along the walls. We're one of only two cars in the lot. The road is greasy, slicks of oil reflecting light. We get out and go inside. There's a long counter, and behind it, a haggard man is wiping a coffee cup with a cloth. There's a jukebox at the back, which is currently playing some song from the sixties. The inside is lit by the bright purple neon of the jukebox.

"Take a seat, boys," the man says, and puts down the coffee cup. "What can I get you?"

Oren sticks his hands in the pockets of his jacket. "Is anyone else here?"

"Just you, now. Should be full, but people are scared."

Oren sits in one of the tall chairs. "Coffee, please. Do you have any pie?"

"Just blueberry at the moment."

"How is it?"

"Better than the cherry."

Oren taps his fist against the counter. "Blueberry, then. Please."

The man turns his dark eyes to me.

"Same."

I don't really want to eat, but food might help stabilize my mood. It's worth a shot, at least.

He pours us each a coffee from a pot I suspect has been sitting there for days, and then goes into the kitchen through a set of swinging doors. I turn in my seat, checking the neon-lit parking lot, but no other cars have arrived. It's just us.

"Can we sit somewhere else?" I ask. "I want to be able to see the front door."

"Oh, sure. Okay."

We move to a booth. A few moments later, the man comes back and plonks down two plates with big slices of blueberry pie on them, along with whipped cream and ice cream. For an empty diner that seems pretty bleak from the outside, this pie looks incredible.

"That's the look I want to see," says the man. "I'll give you two some space. Seems like you've got something to talk about."

He goes back into the kitchen. I take a bite of the pie,

and maybe it's because I haven't been eating much, but it's fucking delicious. I take another big mouthful.

My phone buzzes.

It's from Eli, and it's a picture of Mikey, tied to a chair in the middle of a field.

You have ten minutes before I slit his throat.

Chapter Twenty-Six

Mikey is sitting in front of a TV, but all it's showing is crackling black-and-white static.

The lights are off, so the room is lit by the screen. He remembers he was watching something, but even if he stares directly at the screen, he sees two figures just visible in the static. Their voices are incomprehensible, just quiet murmuring. Distantly, he is aware that he is in a dream, as he hasn't been to this house in years. It's the small home his family rented when they were building their new house when he was a child. For some reason, he always comes back here in his dreams, possibly more often than any other location, even if his family only lived there for a few months.

Mikey gets up and starts making his way through the dark house, sticking close to the walls. He walks cautiously, as if he is expecting someone, or something, to jump out at him at any moment. He leaves the living room, going past the empty dining table and the kitchen, until he reaches the back door. The family cat, Milo, is crying by the door, clearly asking to be let out.

"Hey, buddy," says Mikey. Milo never acts like this. "What's wrong?"

Milo stares at him for a moment before clawing at the door again.

Mikey looks out the window above the kitchen sink and can see that something is going on outside. The air is a thick, hazy red, as if filled with smoke the color of blood. He can smell something burning. A group of armed men runs right past, making him jump. Mikey drops down and hides under the counter. Who the hell was that? Why were they there? What's going on?

In the distance, an explosion sounds. It rocks the entire house. Glasses fall out of a cabinet and smash on the floor. Mikey turns. Milo is scratching at the door frantically now. He can't go out, it's not safe. Something bad is going on out there, and no matter what, he's not going to let Milo face it. Why does he even want to go out there? It's a war zone.

He's—

Mikey's pulled awake. He blinks as the dream, one he's had countless times, vanishes.

The Freak is in front of him.

Mikey tries to move away, but he's too slow, and the Freak injects a needle into the side of his neck. The last thing he sees is the Freak reaching toward him.

A slap on the cheek wakes Mikey.

His head feels foggy. It takes him a few seconds to remember what happened, but as soon as he does, panic sets in. The Freak caught him. He tries to move, but his arms and legs are bound to an office chair by cords of rope. He pulls at them as hard as he can, but they're too tight. He lifts his head and sees the Freak standing in front of him, watching. He comes to his senses more and starts pulling at his bonds wildly, bucking as hard as he can. With resignation he accepts that he isn't going anywhere. He can't get out of this. They're in a sports field somewhere on campus—and nobody else is around. People don't go out on campus at night, not anymore. He figures out where he is. He's in the middle of the lacrosse field. In the distance are the bleachers and the spotlights, which are turned off now.

The Freak is busy sending a message.

Panic takes over again, and Mikey starts to scream for help while pulling at the bindings on his wrists as hard as he can. The Freak steps closer, brandishing the knife, pointing the sharp end of the knife at Mikey's chest.

"Quiet."

Mikey presses himself up against the back of the chair, trying to get as far away from the Freak as he possibly can. It's not far enough, and he feels helpless. It would be so easy for the Freak to kill him right now. All he would need to do is position the blade above his heart and push it in. The Freak flicks his wrist, and the point of the knife slices across Mikey's chest, drawing blood. Agony rolls across his body like a wave as a steady stream of red blood runs down his chest.

"Let me go," says Mikey, his tone turning into a plea. "Please, I don't want to die."

"You might not."

The Freak shows Mikey his phone, and the message that he has sent to Sam.

You've got ten minutes.

The Freak grabs a rag from the pocket of his leather jacket and shoves it into Mikey's mouth, silencing him. Mikey changes his tactic and tries to find the stare of the person underneath the horrific mask. He thinks if he can just get the person, whoever he is, to see his humanity, then he won't go through with his plan. Mikey starts to hyper-ventilate and pulls at the ropes again. He's pulled so hard he's abrased both wrists, and wet flakes of skin are stuck to the rope.

Mikey realizes what the figure in the mask is doing. He's *enjoying* himself. He wants this. He wants his panic, he wants him scared for his life. Whoever this person is, he's pure evil. Mikey changes his tactic once more and glares at the killer. With the gag in his mouth he can't say anything, but he tries to communicate as best he can with his eyes. He hates this man. He hates him more than he has ever hated anyone, or anything.

The Freak pats him on the head, like a dog.

"Eight minutes."

Chapter Twenty-Seven

"He's sent me a location," I say to Fukuda.

I'm in Oren's car, and he's speeding back toward campus. It's probably over the speed limit, but there aren't any cars around, and we only have a few minutes to try to save Mikey's life.

"Send it to me," she says.

Oren goes over a speed bump, and the car lifts up, then bangs down hard onto the road, so hard that both Oren and I jerk forward. I send her the location.

"McDougall's nearby," she says. "I'll send him over."

I check the message Eli sent, and we got it three minutes ago. That was how long it took to get us into the car and on the road. We didn't pay for the food at the diner; that's the least of our worries right now. We just got up and ran out. None of that matters. The only thing that does is getting to Mikey before anything can happen to him.

Even though Oren is quiet, I can tell how worried he is. He's gripping the steering wheel so tight his knuckles have turned bone white. He puts his foot down on the gas, and then off again as we swerve around a corner.

"It's straight ahead," I say.

Through the windshield, the sports grounds of the university come into view. I check the location Eli sent me, and he's there. He must be on the field. What is he doing? We draw closer, and I can see Mikey sitting on a chair in the middle of the field. The field is lit by large lights in the distance, and while there are plenty of places to hide, the only person visible is Mikey.

Oren slams on the breaks and pulls off his seat belt. I take off mine and get out of the car.

I sense movement, and then there's the sound of a body banging up against Oren's car. I run around to the driver's side and see the Freak pinning Oren up against the door. Oren is fighting him with everything he has, and is just managing to keep the knife away from his neck. I take my Taser out of my pocket and charge forward, ready to jam it into him.

The Freak turns and jumps back, away from the Taser. Oren coughs and splutters. The Freak tilts his head to the side as he starts advancing on me.

"Hello, Sam."

"You want me?" I say. "Fucking go for it."

The Freak lunges forward, and I recoil as terror overwhelms me. But it was just a fake-out. The Freak laughs, the sound becoming something demonic because of the voice-changing device he's using.

"You're such a liar," says the Freak. "I'm looking forward to carving your pretty face off."

I start taking slow steps back. Oren is on the ground, clutching his neck, but he doesn't seem to have been cut.

"Try," I say, as I readjust my grip on the Taser. "What are you waiting for?"

"Good question."

The Freak advances, knife at the ready.

"Freeze!"

Sparks fly up from a car to the left of the Freak. He turns and runs toward the rows of parked cars, ducking down low so he's out of sight.

"Sam," says McDougall. Up close, it's clear how young he is: He could only be in his mid-twenties. "Are you okay?"

"Get him!"

McDougall steels himself, then starts making his way toward the rows of cars. I rush up to Oren. The skin around his neck has turned blood red, but I was right before: He hasn't been cut.

"Mikey," says Oren, his voice raspy. "Go, I'm fine."

"Get in the car."

I help him to his feet and back into his car. He locks the doors behind him. Farther in the lot, McDougall is still searching using a flashlight. *Mikey.* I run across the road, toward the field, and sprint as fast as I can until I reach Mikey. He stares back at me, his eyes filled with fear. I reach forward and pull the gag from his mouth.

Back in the lot, a gun goes off. It fires once, then again.

Fuck.

The ropes binding Mikey's wrists are tied incredibly tight. I try to get the first one undone, but I can't. I can't get frustrated, though. Mikey needs me.

"Hurry!" says Mikey. "He might come back!"

I try again, and this time I manage to get it undone. I move on to the next one, and achieve the same, then do the ones binding his ankles. Once the last one is undone, Mikey stands up but then collapses into me. I manage to catch him, holding him upright.

We both watch as an entire squadron of police cars appears.

I remember the gunshots.

Those officers might not be needed. Eli might be gone already. All of this might be over.

I help Mikey back to the lot. As we walk, a whole slew of emotions hits. The terror is still raging within me, but now I can't help but think about Eli. How sweet he was. How much he loved cuddles and said I was his cuddle battery, and how he functioned best when he was given an adequate number of cuddles each day. There's no way Eli could talk to me like the Freak just did.

It's impossible.

I don't know what is going on, but I know it's not him under the mask. Somehow, it's somebody else. They must've faked the picture or something. I don't know. I just know with absolute certainty that the person I was talking to then wasn't Eli.

We reach the lot, and I see Fukuda. She's crying.

I turn and see why.

McDougall is on the ground, covered in knife marks. Whoever killed him was frenzied, as there are dozens of bloody stab wounds across his body, and his face has been caved in so it's a mess of red and white. If I didn't know it was him, he'd be unrecognizable.

"Did you catch him?" I ask.

Fukuda shakes her head.

Chapter Twenty-Eight

I hit the punching bag as hard as I can.

I'm not even going for the proper form that Oren taught me. Not anymore. I don't have the time for that. I just want to hurl my fists at this bag as hard as I can. I punch, and punch again. The respite is only slight, because fury and frustration are taking over. I'm helpless, and now I'm an animal cornered. I want to rip the Freak apart for what he's done. Last night, he killed McDougall, and almost killed Oren, and me and Mikey.

I punch, and replay my conversation with him. It's not Eli under the mask. He could never be so cruel as to say those things to me. There's no chance in the world of that being the case. I don't know what is going on, but I know it's not him.

I hit the bag again. And again. My fist rolls forward upon impact, and pain flares in my wrist. I hiss and move away and start waving my hand through the air. Once the pain has calmed down, I check my wrist, prodding it with the fingers of my other hand. It's a little tender but otherwise fine. The pain is already manageable.

I grab my water bottle and take a drink. If it truly was Eli under the mask, why would he disguise his voice? The only reason he seems to be doing all of this is to make me suffer. Wouldn't hearing his voice, the one I used to love so much, make my suffering worse? Why wear a mask at all? It just doesn't line up, no matter how hard I try to make it fit.

There is only one thing about this that points to it being Eli: the camera footage.

Eli was in the park, in the Freak's mask. They caught him red-handed. He killed Brian, and then they managed to catch him on a security camera taking off his mask. There's no way that could be faked.

I start getting a headache. It's that damn camera footage. If it didn't exist, I would know for sure it wasn't him. But it does, and it's impossible to ignore. It could be photoshopped or altered by some high-level doctoring, but that seems implausible. I should apply Occam's razor to this. What's the simplest solution?

It's that Eli isn't the person I thought he was. Maybe he was faking the whole time that he was with me.

I hit the punching bag again.

Because I don't understand him, I don't have any way of knowing what he will do next. I do know he's getting bolder. So what happens after this? Will he attack another boy? Or maybe he will change tactics and go after my family? I have no way of knowing, no way of predicting what he will do, and that makes me helpless.

It's a dark thought, but after what happened to McDougall, I think the cops might work harder. Clearly what they have been doing hasn't been enough. But now he has killed one of their own.

I punch the bag again, imagining myself hitting the Freak in the face. Even through the mask, the hit would be hard enough to break his nose. That isn't enough for him, not after what he's done. I'm not even sure that jail will be, either. What, he gets to live the rest of his life after he has killed so many, and deeply traumatized a whole group of others? It's not fair. None of this is.

The door to the gym opens, and I stop. I've worked up a sweat, and I have to breathe heavily to get in enough air. Oren walks inside and quickly sets his sights on me. He makes his way over, and I return my attention to the bag.

"I thought you'd be here," he says.

I ignore him and hit the bag again. It's midmorning, and Oren's been spending the day at the house, with Mikey. Both he and Mikey were discharged quickly from the hospital, as both of their injuries were deemed superficial. Physically that is correct, but this will undoubtedly have a long mental impact on them.

"How are you feeling?" I ask.

"Helpless. You?"

"Same."

"He was so fast," says Oren. "If you hadn't interrupted him, he would've killed me."

"I know."

"You can't keep playing the game with him."

"I know. I'm not going to."

"Good." Oren swings his arms. "Do you want to come to the house? Mikey wants to see you."

I catch the bag, stopping it from swinging. He can't be serious. Why would Mikey want to see me? He hated me even before this, and he must hate me even more now. He probably wants me to come to the house just to lose his shit. Even though that doesn't sound even slightly fun, I know I need to go. I owe Mikey that much.

"All right," I say.

Mikey is sitting in the backyard, drinking a beer, surrounded by his brothers. The vibe is mellow, and the yard smells like beer and freshly mown grass. Someone has blown up a kiddie pool, and Booker is sitting in it, smoking a joint. Mikey notices me and lowers his beer. All right, here it comes.

"Let's give them some space," says Oren.

A few brothers mumble complaints, but they all leave the backyard to go inside. Even Booker, who hastily scrubs his trunks with a faded old towel before going in. I sit down beside Mikey.

"Beer?" he asks.

"No thanks."

"Suit yourself." He takes a long drink of his beer and then sits up. "I'm sorry, Sam."

Wait, what?

"Sorry for what?"

"I've been a dick to you this whole time." He takes another drink. "I was jealous and immature, and I'm sorry."

I . . . I don't know how to process this. I was bracing myself for a berating, and this is unexpected.

"You don't have to apologize," I say.

"I do. You've been nothing but nice to everyone, and I was an asshole. Truth is, I think a part of me still has feelings for Oren, and I couldn't handle the way he was looking at you. Still, I shouldn't have treated you the way I did."

"Do you think you and Oren will get back together?"

"Not anymore."

I see things from his perspective. If he is still into Oren, and Oren started showing interest in me, that must be tough on him. I wouldn't have acted the way he did, but I can understand the emotions behind his actions.

"I know I handled things badly with Oren," he says. "And I guess I realized I'd never get a chance to make it better, and that scares me."

"You should tell him."

"Good advice." He cracks his back. "I know we didn't start things off on good terms, but I'm looking forward to being your brother one day."

"I'm looking forward to that, too."

"Are you sure you don't want to have a beer with me?"

"All right, just one," I say.

"That's the spirit."

He gets up to go over to the cooler. As he does, he puts his hand on my shoulder, gives a light squeeze, then continues on. What he said replays in my mind. He's excited to be my brother one day.

I'd like that.

I'm a little tipsy.

It's probably because I skipped breakfast, but the one beer that I shared with Mikey wound up going straight to my head. When I felt it coming on, I went and found Oren and told him what had happened. About halfway through the beer I had with Mikey, I went back in and told the others that our heart-to-heart was done, and they all came back and started hanging out in the backyard. I told Oren that I want to go to my room, and he drove me back.

Now we're at my door.

"Thanks for driving me back," I say.

"No problem."

"What are you going to do now?"

He scratches his arm. "Probably crash; I'm pretty tired. Would you want to come to my room, though?"

My eyebrows shoot up.

"Not like that!" he yelps. "I just mean, I'd feel safer if I knew where you were. You could nap on my couch if you want."

I actually agree with his logic, and as much as he wants to keep an eye on me, I want to do the same with him.

"Sure," I say.

We go down the hall to his room. He flicks on the light and then closes the door behind him. I take out my Taser and check everywhere someone could be hiding, but there's nobody in here. It's just us. Oren retrieves a pillow and a spare blanket and tosses them onto his couch.

"You can take the bed if you want," he says.

"The couch is fine."

"You sure?"

"Yep."

"Okay. 'Night, Sam."

"'Night."

Chapter Twenty-Nine

I sit up, instantly wide awake.

This keeps happening. Every time I fall asleep, I find myself having terrible nightmares, almost all of which involve the Freak. He's murdered me in countless ways now. I've had my throat slit, been stabbed through the heart, even fallen through a trapdoor into a pit of spikes. Those aren't the worst nightmares, though. The worst of those are when Oren is in my dreams, too, and I have to watch, totally helpless, as the Freak kills him.

Oren and I have spent the day together. For a while we were both awake, and he ordered food to be delivered, and we ate Chinese while watching a movie. Neither of us had energy even for that, though, and about halfway through we decided to go back to sleep. I check my phone. It's nearly nine now, which makes it official. I've slept most of the day away. I don't have any messages, and that's good. Hopefully how close the Freak got to getting caught has spooked him enough to slow down his plans.

Wait.

Every other time I've been awake, I've been able to hear Oren's light snoring. Now the room is completely silent. I get up off the couch and check Oren's bed.

He's not here.

I call him, but he doesn't pick up. "Hey, it's Oren. Leave a message." I pace around the room and try to relax, but I can't. Why would he go out at night? I check Instagram. He's posted a story.

In the story, Oren is outside, standing by the Munroe statue on the quad. He's wearing running gear and making a peace sign. What the hell? I know exactly where he is. If I wanted to find him, I could follow the path and get right to him. He must know he is one of the Freak's biggest targets. He has always been so smart, so what is he doing? It clicks.

He's making himself a target.

But he's underestimating Eli, and he's going to get himself killed.

I call him again. *Come on, pick up, pick up.* No answer.

"Hey, it's Oren. Leave a message."

I text him.

What are you doing????

I try calling him again. Once again, it just rings and rings.

I call Fukuda. She picks up.

"Hello?" she says, her voice taut. Given the demands of her job and the loss of her partner, I've probably woken her, if she's had the luxury of any sleep.

"Sam, what's wrong?"

I'm so panicked I can barely form a coherent sentence. Oren is trying something, and it's not going to work. He would've told me about it if he thought he had a good chance. These are the actions of a desperate person making a gamble.

"I think Oren's in danger," I say. "He's set a trap for Eli, and he's making himself bait. He posted a story, and, and—"

"Sam, calm down. Take a breath."

"You need to go to the Munroe statue now."

"Okay, I will. Stay where you are, all right? I'll handle this."

I hang up, then leave the room. Oren on his own stands no chance, and Fukuda might be too slow. But maybe if I can make it to Eli before he finds Oren, then I can stop him. If I stay in my room and the Freak finds Oren, then he's as good as dead.

I run out the door and down the hallway to the elevator. I jab the button a few times. *Hurry up . . .*

The doors finally open. I rush inside, then press the ground button and jam the door close button. Nothing is going fast enough. Oren is out there, with Eli. He's going to die because of me.

The doors open, and I sprint out. I run across the campus. My lungs start to burn, but I push through the pain. Nobody else is dying because of me. If the Freak wants me, he can have me, but he isn't going to hurt Oren.

I reach the statue and peer around. There's nobody here. I check Instagram, and Oren has posted a second story. He's in Toohey Park, where Brian was killed. I can see the entrance from here, cast in darkness from towering trees. It's all too similar to the woods that surrounded the lake house.

I don't have a choice. He's out there, I know it. Both of them are.

Forcing down my nerves, I run into the park. The moon is almost full, and the park is lit by iron streetlights. The trees cast long shadows, and I see shapes in them. I look around, trying to sense movement. It's so dark, though, that it's hard to make out anything. I have to go deeper. I can't stop.

A branch snaps somewhere in the trees, and I turn around. But there's nobody there, at least not that I can see.

"Help!"

It's Oren's voice, farther on. He sounds distant. Too distant.

I run faster. I go around a corner, and I see them. Oren is wrestling with the Freak. Oren headbutts him, and then pushes him off and scrambles to his feet.

"Now!" shouts Oren.

Around the pair, figures emerge from the darkness, stepping out from behind trees. There are dozens of them, and each of them is wearing a Halloween mask and holding a weapon of some sort: There are baseball bats, knives, even knuckle-dusters. A lot of them are wearing shirts with our Greek letters across the chest. The Freak turns from side to side and starts to take small steps backward. He's knows he has lost, and that he is now the prey.

"Get him," says Oren.

The Freak tries to run, but the group has already encircled him. They close in, and this feels familiar. I've felt this before, if only for a second. It's the desire to kill.

This is different, though. I had to kill. But there's nowhere for the Freak to go from here. He's surrounded.

"Wait!" calls the Freak. "Stop!"

A boy in a clown mask gets brave and tries to hit the Freak with the baseball bat he's holding. The Freak dodges. A different brother strikes the Freak in the back of the head with a large steel ornament, and the Freak stumbles forward. Sensing their chance, the others descend and start striking with ferocity. The Freak tries to get up, but Oren kicks him in the head, and he slumps to the ground, limp. That doesn't stop them, and they keep attacking. I already know I can't control them, a sort of group mentality has taken over.

They're going to beat him to death.

"Stop!" I shout, and I grab Oren by the shirt and pull him away. I see bloodlust in his eyes. He'll calm down and come back to himself soon, he just needs a second. This will pass, once the fear is out of his system.

"You don't know what you're doing," I say.

"Yes, I do."

He tries to get past me, but I stop him.

"Don't do this," I say.

"You did!" he shouts.

I go still.

The frenzy in his eyes evaporates. "Sam, I didn't mean that."

"Sam!" shouts the Freak.

The Freak crawls forward and raises his hand, begging for help.

A gunshot sounds, and everyone pauses.

Officer Fukuda is standing on the path, her gun raised high into the air. I don't think I've ever been as relieved to see someone. This is good. The Freak is in bad shape, but he's alive. I will kill again if I need to, but he's helpless at the moment. That's the difference between what I did and murder. I've always known that, but now I believe it.

"Move," says Fukuda.

The masked people start taking off their masks. Now I recognize more of them. They're the brothers and pledges of Alpha Phi Nu. Fukuda approaches the Freak, her gun aimed at him.

"Wait," says Oren. "Sam should do it."

Do what? But then I see Fukuda is kneeling in front of the Freak, her hand on his mask. What if it isn't Eli under there? The thought brings me a tiny flicker of hope. Maybe Eli isn't a killer.

Fukuda backs away.

"If he moves," I say, "shoot."

I don't want to see this. But I know I have to. One way or another, I am going to get my answer.

I go up to the Freak extremely cautiously. Even though he is still, I don't want to take any chances. Animals are most dangerous when they're trapped. He seems so weak right now. So helpless. But he's not. Whoever is under this mask has been stalking me and is a cold-blooded murderer. He's a sick, twisted monster, a true freak, and he deserves this. He deserves worse, actually. Even if it is Eli, he's not the guy I was in love with; he must've died a long time ago.

I reach down and grip the mask.

I pull it up, and my whole world comes crashing down.

His face is bloody, but still. He's grown a beard, and his hair is no longer dyed black, so it's returned to its natural reddish brown. He's grown it long, so long it needs to be tied back into a ponytail. Even with these changes, it's still him.

It's Eli.

I move backward, holding the mask. Fukuda bends down and roughly pulls Eli's hands behind his back.

"Wait!" he shouts. "I can explain!"

"You're under arrest for the murders of Chris McDougall, Justin Lynch . . ."

"Sam," he says. "I didn't do it, he made me! I'm innocent." He starts to cry. "Please, Sam, I didn't—"

"Quiet," says Fukuda. "Not another word, okay?"

"I'm innocent!"'

Fukuda pulls a now handcuffed Eli to his feet.

"Sam, you know me, I wouldn't do this!"

He's lying, though. He has to be. He was here, we caught him.

He's the killer.

"I hope you rot," I say.

Chapter Thirty

Police are everywhere.

It's an entire platoon, all sitting in their cars in the lot by the entrance to the park. A barricade has been set up, blocking the journalists and nosy students from coming too close. I'm sitting in the back of an ambulance, with a blue woolen blanket wrapped around my shoulders. They've taken Eli away, I'm guessing to the station for interrogation. Good. When he was being driven away, I could sense he was watching me from the back of the station wagon, but I couldn't get myself to look at him.

A paramedic offers me a cup of tea.

"Thanks," I say as I take it. I'm not really thirsty, and I've never been a tea person anyway, but it feels nice to hold, warming my cold hands. The other pledges and brothers are being interviewed by officers, but I doubt they'll get much from us. I wonder if the cops will even try to prosecute anyone—they did break the law when they decided to become vigilantes and assault someone. But who can blame them? And, more important, their plan worked. They caught the bad guy. They did what the cops should've done.

Oren, who has been speaking to an officer, notices me. He says something, then starts walking over. He sits down beside me and clasps his hands together.

"I'm sorry," he says. "I should've told you."

I stare into the blackness of my tea. "Why didn't you?"

"I didn't want to give you the chance to talk me out of it."

"That's not a good reason."

"I know. Can you forgive me?"

I think about it. Can I? Sure, his plan worked, they managed to get Eli, and even through everything, I can already feel a massive sense of relief steadily building. Eli is caught. It's over. I can finally have what I wanted, which is a normal life. But still, Oren put himself in such enormous danger to do it, and he went behind my back. What if his plan hadn't worked and someone had died?

"I can't answer that right now. I need time."

"I understand." He swallows. "About what he said . . ."

"He was lying," I say. "I know."

The truth is . . . a little more complicated than that. I wish I could completely believe that he was lying. But I can't. There's still a part of me, a small part, sure, but it's still there, that thinks Eli might've been telling the truth. He said that someone made him do what he was doing. It is what the Freak has been doing to me, so is it completely impossible that the true Freak did the same thing to Eli?

Or maybe Eli knows this, too. Maybe he knows that saying what he did is the best way to make sure that I never have peace, because I won't until the Freak is caught. Maybe Eli said what he did because he knew it was the best way possible to hurt me, even if he did get captured. It's possible this is his backup plan. Surely he has one, because he has always managed to stay ahead of the cops, which makes me think that he has a carefully constructed plan.

"Sam!" calls a voice. It's Mom, and she's pushed her way to the front of the crowd of onlookers. She goes under the barricade and comes up to me. "I heard. I . . ."

She tries to hug me, but I pull back. Beside me, Oren tenses.

"What are you doing here?" I ask.

"You're my son, I—"

"Go!" I shout.

I am sure that she's lying. She isn't here to see me, there is no way. She is here because this is a pivotal scene in the story. This is the conclusion. The killer has been captured, and she wants to be here. She probably has a notebook in her handbag and is writing small details she sees in order to make her book seem as real as possible.

Fukuda jogs over. "What's wrong?"

"Can you make her leave?" I ask.

"I just want to support you," says Mom. Her bottom lip is trembling. It's an act, it has to be. I doubt she's capable of crying over anything but herself.

"Bullshit!" I shout.

"Easy," says Fukuda. "Sam, calm down."

"Don't tell me to calm down! Please, get rid of her, I don't want to see her."

"I'll leave," says Mom. "But, Sam, I really did come here for you."

"Get the fuck away from me."

Her mouth drops open, but then she turns and walks away, back toward the crowd. I think if I wasn't already emotionally overloaded by what's happened tonight, I would cry. I would totally lose it. In its place is this numbness. I've felt too much recently so that my body has just switched off my emotions as a defense mechanism.

"My mother's a nightmare, too," says Fukuda. "She didn't talk to me for a year when I told her I was going to be a cop."

I sip my tea.

"Do you want me to take you back to your dorm?" she asks.

"Yes, please." I stand, then turn to Oren. "Are you coming?"

"Later. You go."

Fukuda leads me to her police car, and I get in.

She drives slowly, taking us through the crowd, which

parts in front of us. They all stare, or film. This will be all over the news soon, if it isn't already. It's not a long drive back to the dorm, but I'm thankful to be in the car, so I don't get hounded on the way there.

She parks in front of the dorm. All the journalists have remained with the ambulances and police cars by the entrance to the parking lot, so it's quiet here.

"Would you like me to walk you to your room?" she asks.

I consider it, but then change my mind. Why should I? I have no reason to need constant company anymore. Eli's been captured.

"I'm fine," I say. "Thanks for the lift."

"Stay safe."

"You too."

I get back to my room and open the door. I do my usual routine, making sure it's empty, then drop down onto my bed. My thoughts swirl.

Eli's been caught.

It's over.

Chapter Thirty-One

"So hi," says Beth. "It's time, once again, for *Margaritas and Murder*. I'm Beth Jones, and I've been giving you a firsthand account of what it's been like to live through a murder spree. And guys, it happened. The killer was caught. Last night, a group of brothers from the Alpha Phi Nu fraternity put together a trap and managed to catch the killer, eighteen-year-old Eli Mattherson. It's over, everyone."

She inserts the sound of a crowd cheering.

"Now, don't think this is going to be the end of my coverage, by any means. I'm going to have interviews with some of the brothers, including one I'm recording this afternoon, which I will upload the second that I can. Trust me, you guys, this is only just the beginning. I'll be covering the court case, and of course I will try my best to get an interview with the man of the hour, Sam Carville."

I pause the podcast and take off my headphones. That's enough of that for this early in the morning. That's enough of that for a whole lifetime, if I'm being totally honest.

I shouldn't judge, though. If the way Beth processes this

is by recording a podcast, then who am I to judge her for that. Eli killed her boyfriend, so I think she can do whatever she wants.

Everything feels slightly forced, but the resounding feeling that has come over the campus is relief. We got an email this morning saying that a memorial service for the slain has been organized for the weekend, and classes are expected to start. In addition, any Munroe student who wishes will get access to a psychologist if they want to. I get up and go over to the window and peer out. The quad is filled with people, busier than I've seen it since this all started. There are a few news crews out there, but for the most part it's just people trying to move on and to get back some sense of normalcy that was taken from them. I check my phone, and I have a new message from a group chat called ΑΦΝ Pledges. The message is from a brother named Jerome, who I have seen around but haven't really spoken to.

Hey pledges! We're organizing a party tonight in honor of Tripp, Brian, and Justin. As pledges, it is your duty to get the house ready, so be here in an hour, and get ready to clean.

A short while later, I'm in the bathroom of the frat house, scrubbing the sink. Drew is the only pledge who has been allowed to skip this, for obvious reasons. He's out of the hospital and has been encouraged to take it easy, but I've heard that he's planning on coming tonight. He says he wouldn't miss it for anything.

"This is bullshit," says Booker as he scrubs the toilet. "We survive a massacre, and this is how they thank us?"

I scoff, and continue scrubbing the sink.

"Faster!" shouts a voice. I look over my shoulder and see Jerome standing in the doorway. He has volunteered to take over as president from Tripp, and so far, I'd say he's doing a great job. Even if he makes us clean up an entire frat house.

"Just think," says Jerome. "When you're brothers, you'll get your pledges to do this. You missed a spot, Carville."

He points, and I have missed a spot. I scrub it as Jerome walks away.

"Have you heard about Josh?" asks Booker.

"No?"

"He's coming back. He's not coming to the party tonight, but he's coming back to campus. He said something about recording a podcast with Beth."

I keep scrubbing, harder than before.

"Would you ever go on her show?" asks Booker. "I've been reading the comments, and everyone wants you to."

I mull it over. Because of the murders, and her closeness to them, Beth's podcast has become a juggernaut success. It's now in the top ten of the podcast charts, and she's had coverage in places like *The New York Times*. She is kind of famous now.

"Should I?" I ask.

"Depends on how much she pays you."

I tap on the side of my nose, as someone else comes into the doorway. It's Oren. I get a sugar rush, but then I look past him and see Fukuda. My stomach plummets. Whatever she's here for? It can't be good.

"What happened?" I ask.

"Nothing," she says. "But I need your help. Eli isn't talking. He said the only person he'll say anything to is you. I want your help one last time, Sam."

I lean against the sink. Eli probably just wants to tell me the story he started before, to make sure I have doubts about him. I'm on to him now. I know he's just trying to make sure I never relax again. And he doesn't scare me. If what he wants is to talk to me, I'll talk to him, and get a confession from him.

Then I never have to see him again.

"How are you feeling?" asks Fukuda.

We're at the station, walking toward the interrogation room, where Eli is being kept.

"I just want to get this over with," I say. "He's really not talking to anyone?"

"Nope, not even his lawyer. He's written down that the only person he'll speak to is you."

"Okay. Is there anything I should do to get a confession out of him?"

"Just get him talking. He's going to confess; my theory is he wants you to be the person he confesses to."

I take that in. He probably enjoys this as much, too. Given what he has been doing, there's no way that he could have expected to get away with this as long as he did. He's probably disappointed that he didn't manage to kill me before Oren and the rest of the brotherhood outwitted him. Maybe I'll rub that in.

Fukuda leads me down a hallway and stops outside a door, clearly leading to an interrogation room. I feel the urge to run as quickly as I can from this place. I don't want to see him. In fact, it's maybe the last thing on earth I would want to do. But I am not running anymore.

I'm ending this, once and for all.

I go inside.

Eli is sitting at the table, his hands cuffed and bound to the table. He has a nasty bruise on his left eye and a split lip.

Eli's mouth twists. "Are you going to sit?"

I carefully move to the chair and pull it out.

"I'm not going to attack you," he says, moving his hands as far as the chains will allow, to demonstrate how he can't move very far.

"Fuck you," I say. "I'll do what I want."

"I know."

"Why did you want to talk to me?" I ask. "Tell me so I can go."

He glances at the door.

I cross my arms. "Go on. Confess."

"I was set up, Sam. I know you don't believe me, but it's true."

"You're lying."

Desperation fills is eyes. "Please, listen to me. I didn't do this. He captured me and kept me in his basement. He told me what to do, and as long as I did what he asked, he said he wouldn't kill you."

"You killed to protect me?"

"No, Sam, no. I didn't kill anyone. He told me to go into the park twice. That's all I've done. I didn't know anyone had died. He took my phone."

"Why didn't you run when he let you out?"

"He said he'd kill you. Please, you have to believe me." He breaks down and starts crying. "It wasn't me."

He strains against his cuffs, trying to get as close as possible. I lean back. I don't want to be anywhere near him.

The Eli I knew is long gone. Whoever this person is, he's just trying to mess with me.

"Please," he says. "You know me. You know I wouldn't do this."

"You're wrong, I don't know you."

I can already see where this is going. He isn't going to confess. This is all just part of his act. But I've got places to be and a party to get ready for tonight.

"You're not safe!" says Eli. "Sam, wait, listen to me!"

I'm done doing that. I get up and leave.

Chapter Thirty-Two

"I'm here with Munroe Massacre survivor Josh Stargensky," says Beth. "Why don't you introduce yourself, Josh?"

They're sitting in a podcast recording studio, a room near the back of the library. It's available 24/7 and is open to anyone, so it's not really anyone's studio. One of the walls is covered in purple and black soundproofing. All the equipment, too, is top-of-the-line. The desk has an iMac, as well as a pretty solid microphone.

"Er, hi," says Josh. "I'm Josh, and I'm a film major and Alpha Phi Nu pledge."

"Welcome, Josh. I know my listeners have been so eager to talk to some of the brothers, so I'm delighted to have you here."

"Thanks for having me."

"I've gotten a lot of questions from my listeners, so I think we should dive right into it. Does that sound good?"

"I'm ready," says Josh.

"Until next time," says Beth. "Don't go down any dark alleys! Good night."

She presses the button on the computer, and the recording stops.

"We're done?" asks Josh.

"We sure are," says Beth.

"Sweet. How was it?"

She checks a note on her desk. "Good. My listeners are going to love it."

Josh notices that her tone slightly changed just then, becoming a little less warm than she did while they were still recording. It's probably nothing, he tells himself. She's a performer, of course she uses most of her energy while she's working.

"Are you going to the party?" she asks.

Josh has considered it and decided against it. While he does feel like this is over, because the killer has been caught, he has seen too many horror movies to go to a party like that. They're generally a bloodbath. No, he has decided that he will sit out parties for the foreseeable future. He is not going to walk down any dark alleyways, and he's not going anywhere by himself for a long time. There is always a sequel to be afraid of, too, and he does not want to be the opening kill in Munroe Massacre 2, that's for sure.

"You can go," says Beth.

He waits, wrapping his fingers around the strap of his satchel.

"He's been caught, Josh. It's over."

"I know, I just . . . don't want to go anywhere by myself now."

"Do you want me to walk you to your car?"

"Yes, please."

"Ugh."

She starts packing up her stuff and then pulls out her pepper spray. Josh waits, not wanting to open the door. She rolls her eyes and opens it. She stops for a moment, pulls a horrified face, and ducks back inside and slams the door.

"What?" asks Josh. "Is he there?"

"No. It's just books."

She opens the door again, chuckling to herself.

"That's not funny," he says, his voice strangled.

The two go out. The recording studios are on the second level of the library, which is now pretty quiet. There's a librarian working at a desk on the first level, but everyone else seems to have left. They're probably at the party. Most of the school is going; it's expected to be a blowout along the entire Greek Row. Josh regrets his choice now, because even if parties are a bloodbath in horror movies, that's only after the people have all left early, generally for a convenient reason, or the killer shepherds them out. Or a body is discovered and everyone runs away screaming.

Beth gasps.

From a row of books, the Freak has emerged.

Josh replays each horror movie he's seen. Every time he's wanted to scream at a character to stop being an idiot and *run*. He's not going to make that mistake, because he actually has some brain cells. He's not going to try to face the killer. He isn't going to try to fight him head-on. He isn't going to do anything other than put as much distance between him and the monster as he can.

The Freak pulls out a knife.

Josh's stare moves down to the silver blade of the knife, all the way to the pointed end. He's seen people in this exact situation countless times, but he's never felt anything close to this. It's pure fear, making the fine hairs on his arms rise, and his hands and feet start to feel cold. A scream is caught in his throat, and his mind is urging him to run, but he knows he is being cornered by a predator, and if he turns, the chase will begin.

The Freak runs forward. Beth and Josh turn and sprint as fast as they can back the way they came. Josh keeps running as Beth trips, and the Freak reaches her. She screams as the Freak plunges his knife into her back.

Josh reaches the recording studio and tries the door. It's locked. He turns back to see the Freak stand up at full height. On the ground, Beth is totally still, with a deep wound in her back. Josh gives up on the door and runs.

"Help!"

He reaches a study room, which is a dead end. He looks around, but there's no way out, and nowhere for him to go. The Freak is right behind him. Josh picks up a chair and holds it out in front of him.

The Freak advances.

Josh tosses the chair at the Freak as hard as he can, but the Freak closes the distance. Josh is frustrated at himself for a second before the Freak's knife is plunged deep into his stomach. There's an impact, like a punch to the gut, and then he feels it inside him, solid metal touching his organs. Josh gasps as the knife twists and blood surges up his windpipe. He coughs, and flecks of red splatter across the Freak's mask.

The Freak steps away, and Josh falls. The Freak grabs him by the hair and pulls him across the floor to the row of desks against a wall. The Freak unplugs one of the computers, then bends down, wraps the black cord around Josh's neck and pulls it tight.

Josh knows it's too late.

He's seen this happen so many times. He's witnessed thousands of deaths.

Now it's his turn.

Chapter Thirty-Three

I look up at AΦN house.

Everyone has been saying that this will be the biggest party that Munroe University has ever seen, and from the looks of things right now, it is. It's not even 6:00 P.M. and the house is already full of people. Loud music is blaring from inside, and groups of people are crowded around the entrance, waiting to get in. Jerome had an idea to make it a ticketed event, in order to raise money for not only the families of Tripp, Brian, and Justin, but for all the victims. It costs twenty dollars to attend, and as long as everyone who is here has paid, then those families should get a small fortune.

A police car is parked out front, and Fukuda is leaning against it. I go up to her.

"You know there's underage drinking in there, right?" I ask.

She smiles. "I'll let it slide, just this once."

"Are you going to come in?"

She laughs and shakes her head. "My wife would never let me hear the end of it if I went to a frat party."

"Fair enough. Has Eli said anything else?"

"He's sticking to his story, but it won't hold up. He's going to be in jail for the rest of his life." Fukuda notices something at the front of the house. "I think your friends want you."

I turn, and Drew is in the doorway, waving at me.

"Have fun," she says. "You deserve it."

I push my way through the crowd, until I make it up to Drew.

"Hey!" says a guy in line who we have pushed in front of. "Why does he get to cut in?"

I turn around.

"Oh," says the guy. "Sorry, carry on."

I buy my ticket and am given a red paper wristband. Inside is even more crowded than I had imagined, and the music is so loud. People are cramped body to body and have made a dance floor out of the living room. From the top stairwell, a brother cracks open a bottle of champagne and sprays it out onto the awaiting crowd.

"Wild, right?" asks Drew.

"I love it."

"We should get you a drink," he says.

We push our way through to the kitchen. Every free part of counter space is loaded with drinks. Booker is in the kitchen, sipping from a Solo cup.

"Sam!" he says.

He throws his arms around me and hugs me tight. I squeeze him to my chest. Like always, he smells like weed, but it's not bad. Maybe one day he could teach me how to smoke. I might like that.

"What do you feel like?" asks Drew.

"Vodka."

"Nice. Want to do shots?"

"Sure."

He clears some counter space and pours the three of us a shot. I pick mine up and have a moment of hesitation. If Eli was telling the truth, then it isn't a good idea to get drunk. I ignore the thought and take the shot. It burns, but in a good way. This is what I should've been doing this whole time. I shouldn't have had to go through the entire nightmare that I did. I'm eighteen. I should be at a frat party, getting drunk, and making choices I might regret later. I should hook up with a cute guy simply because I want to.

But there's only one guy who I want to hook up with.

I take out my phone and text him. Even if he did keep his plan a secret from me, I forgive him.

Hey, I'm here, where are you?

"Another?" asks Booker.

Drew doesn't even wait for our responses before he pours each of us a new shot.

"Are you doing shots?"

It's Alyson.

"Want to join?" I ask.

She comes closer, and Drew pours her a shot, too. Booker counts down, then we all do the shot.

"Can we talk?" I ask Alyson.

"I'll be back," I say to Drew and Booker.

I follow Alyson through the party, to the backyard. At the side of the house is the outdoor seating area where I had my talk with Mikey. Most of the chairs are taken, but Alyson finds two that are free.

"Some party, huh?" says Alyson.

"Yeah."

"This all really suits you, Sam," she says. "You were, like, born to be a frat boy."

"Thank you?"

"You're welcome."

"I'm really sorry for the way I treated you," I say. "I miss you. I just needed to heal for a while. I should've told you that."

"You should've. I would've been there for you, if you'd asked me."

"I know, and it would've helped. I'm sorry I didn't."

"It's okay. Do you think maybe you want to try being friends again?"

"So you forgive me?" I ask.

"Bygones."

I drum my fingers on my legs. "Want to dance?"

"Yes."

We walk back to the dance floor, and I check my phone. Oren still hasn't responded. I don't think he's ever taken this long to respond before. What is he doing? I don't want to go down this rabbit hole. I'm sure he's fine, he's probably just busy. Alyson and I reach the dance floor, just when "Yeah!" by Usher starts to play. Alyson rolls her eyes, because yeah, this song is maybe a little on the nose, but there's no denying that it is a bop. The chorus hits, and I throw my hands up into the air.

Alyson and I dance for a few songs, but I keep thinking about Oren. For him to not respond is weird.

"I'll be back," I tell Alyson.

I leave the dance floor and make it to a hallway that's at least got enough space to take my phone out. I check my messages, and Oren still hasn't responded. He isn't here, he . . .

He's right in front of me.

He makes his way forward, and grabs my shirt and leads me to the dance floor. We might be surrounded by people right now, but it feels like Oren is the only one here. There are so many people that we are pressed right up against each other, and I'm closer to him than I've ever been. I'm inches from him, one step away from feeling his chest against mine. He gives me a soft smile as his hand reaches out and touches mine. I link my fingers into his and smile back.

I lean in close. "I forgive you," I say.

He nods, then pulls me to him and kisses me. I wrap my arms around his neck and kiss him back. It feels like being inside when it's storming. It feels like I've left my body and I'm floating above the dance floor. It feels like I could live in this moment forever and be completely content.

He ends the kiss and rubs my cheek.

Oren kissed me. He kissed me. He freaking kissed me!

He lowers his hands so they're on my hips. I know I only just kissed him, but I want more.

I lean forward and kiss him.

Somehow, it's even better.

We reach a spare bedroom, and Oren steps closer. He looks different right now, maybe softer than he ever has. His eyes are unblinking and clearly filled with genuine care for me. And maybe something else, too, something primal. He closes the door and then comes back.

I step closer and press my lips to his.

"You sure?" he asks.

I pull him closer, and he kisses me with everything he has. I go completely breathless. This is moving fast, but I want it to. I've lost two years of my life. I can't get them back, but I'm done with playing it safe. I'm not stopping myself from doing what I want now. And what I want is to not stop what I'm doing with Oren.

"We don't have to do this if you don't want to," he says, breathless.

"I know."

He kisses me again, and moves me back so I'm up against the wall. He runs his hand down my chest, over my stomach, to my belt. As he kisses, he starts trying to undo it. I tilt my head back against the cool plaster, and he laughs, resting his head on my shoulder.

"I can't get it," he says.

I undo my belt for him, then undo his. Once they're both undone, he kisses me again, even harder. He presses his body fully up against mine, and the contact is amazing, but I want more. I want his bare skin against mine.

He pulls my shirt off and tosses it away. He touches my chest, and his fingertips run down until they reach the scar above my heart. He brushes over it, then goes down lower, to my belly button. The touch almost makes me shudder, and everywhere he touches sends up sparks. I unbutton his shirt and then start kissing his neck, then down to the soft skin of his chest. He smells fantastic, like his cologne. What strikes me is how natural this feels. Maybe it's just relief that this nightmare is over, but there's no awkwardness right now. And every part of my body wants Oren, and from the looks of things, he wants me just as badly.

"I have condoms," he says.

He leans in close and whispers what he wants me to do to him.

"Wow," I say.

He laughs. "I'll take that as a yes?"

I wrap my arms around him. "*Yes.*"

Turns out, having sex on a single bed is pretty difficult.

There is so little space to really move around. Not that I'm complaining. Oren and I have moved around a few times, and now we've finally found a position that should work. He's underneath me, his cheeks flushed from kissing. We're both naked, we took off our underwear before climbing into bed, but I don't feel at all self-conscious.

"Ready?" I ask.

He pulls me to him, and kisses me again. I move a little closer, and he wraps his legs around me, and suddenly we're so close. I watch him, and he lets out a soft moan. It's maybe the hottest thing I've ever seen.

"Sam," he says.

I can't believe I'm doing this.

I press forward, and my thoughts start to go blank, as sensations spread across my whole body.

Once I feel myself come back to reality, I kiss Oren on the top of the head, and then roll over to the side.

"Holy shit," he says. He puts a hand behind his head, getting comfortable.

"Yeah."

Now that the frenzy of sex has passed, I realize what I've done. Not that, I mean, I know we just had sex. *Incredible* sex.

"What's wrong?" asks Oren.

"Nothing."

He narrows his eyebrows. "Talk to me."

"Should we have done that?"

He sits up and puts his hand on my chest. "You didn't want to?"

"No, I did. I just . . . We haven't even gone out yet."

He laughs softly. "We have plenty of time for that. But right now . . ."

He starts kissing my neck.

"Already?" I ask.

"That a problem for you, Carville?"

Something about him saying my last name wipes any worry about that away. Or maybe it's the mocking smile he's giving me. I roll over so I'm on top of him. I stop, and smile back at him.

"What?" he asks, tilting his head to the side.

"Nothing. I'm just happy I met you."

"I'm happy I met you, too."

I press his forearms into the bed and kiss him.

Chapter Thirty-Four

Mikey wants to be happy for Oren.

He really does.

It's hard, though. Because while he knows that he didn't really handle the situation with Oren well, he tried his best. And he hoped that maybe, one day, he and Oren would get back together, once both of them have done some growing. That never seemed to be in any danger until Sam showed up and made everything so much messier. And even if Mikey did fix things with Sam, he's still not over Oren. He doubts that he will ever be over Oren. How does one get over a boy that incredible? It doesn't seem possible.

"What are you waiting for?" asks Jerome. "Throw."

Mikey blinks and is pulled out of his daze. The frat party is going on around him, and this is easily the biggest of any that Mikey has been to, and that's saying something, as he's been to a lot of historic parties.

He throws the table tennis ball, and it bounces once, then goes into the cup on the other end.

The crowd of brothers around him cheers, but Mikey

isn't really feeling it. He saw Oren and Sam retreat to a spare bedroom a short time ago, even though the party is still going. They're probably having sex, he assumes. And that means that Oren is off-limits, because Oren is a one-man kind of guy. He hasn't heard any word of him even hooking up in all the time he's been single. Harrison's death did change Oren a lot, he used to be a lot more carefree, but Mikey doubts that Oren would suddenly change that part of him.

He knows this isn't Sam's fault. It's his. Oren needed him, and he couldn't be there for him, because he was finding the schoolwork way more intense than he was expecting, so he had a million things that he felt he needed to be focusing on, and Oren and his grief was a complication that he eventually decided he didn't want to deal with anymore.

He can't believe how selfish he was. Oren is the sweetest, most incredible guy, and he lost his little brother. And Mikey wasn't man enough to stand by him. He was too selfish and cared too much about everything that had been going on in his own life at the time to stand by him. There's no coming back from that in terms of a relationship. How could Oren ever be with him again, knowing how he acted? Oren could never fully trust him again.

Mikey wonders what tonight would be like if things between him and Oren hadn't gone sour. They would've been dating for over a year now. He's sure he would be deeply in love with him, even more than he was during their honeymoon period. His life would be better if he had kept Oren as his partner, that much is obvious. The occasional hookup he goes on, while hot, isn't the same. It barely scratches the surface of what he had, and lost.

Mikey decides to make a deal with himself. He'll apologize to Oren for the way he treated him. Maybe then they can be friends. His mind races forward, like maybe being friends will be the first step to them getting back together, but he pushes that thought away. He had his chance with Oren, and he screwed it up. And Oren deserves to be happy, and from the looks of things, Sam makes him happy. The kindest thing he can do now is stay out of the way and let Oren be happy with someone new. If anyone he knows deserves to be happy, it's Oren, after everything he has been through.

"You okay?" asks Drew.

"Yeah, just tired," says Mikey. "I might crash."

"I got stabbed and I'm still going."

"Sorry. 'Night, man."

"'Night."

Mikey pushes through the crowd, who are standing packed together, talking. A couple is up against the wall, making out. Mikey doesn't know either of them but still feels a pang of jealousy. Which is unfounded; he knows he would have no trouble replicating that if that's what he wanted: He could go on an app and have a man at his door in the next half hour. He hates the thought, but he wants to be doing that with Oren.

He ducks under the rope blocking off the stairwell and goes upstairs.

Sam is probably kissing Oren now. Oren's cheeks are probably flushed in that way that happens, which is both incredibly cute and hot. And it should be him, not Sam. Mikey reaches his door and pushes it open to go inside.

He takes out his wallet and keys, and puts them on his desk. Then he kicks off his shoes and drops onto bed.

Oren.

He might've been the love of his life. He might be . . .

There's a noise from under the bed. Mikey frowns. He is drunk, but not so drunk that he's totally out of control of himself. But he is probably just imagining hearing that. Eli was caught, the danger has passed. He has no reason to be afraid right now, or to be scared of something under the bed. He's not a kid anymore.

He hears it again, the floorboards creaking slightly.

Nope, that's it. There's someone under there. And if there isn't, then oh well. He's not going to risk that chance. He would rather look like a fool and not be in any danger than stick around only to get killed.

He knows what he has to do and decides he doesn't want to wait. He moves as quickly as he can and gets up out of bed. He sees a flash of silver from under the bed, and agony erupts. He crashes down. He looks back to see that he has a deep gash across the back of his ankle. Blood spurts from the cut.

Behind him, the Freak moves out from under the bed and stands up at his full height. Mikey scrambles back, until he hits his door.

"Help!" he shouts, as loud as he can.

But he knows he isn't loud enough. He can hear the music from the party drowning him out.

The Freak steps toward Mikey and raises his knife. Mikey watches it plunge into his stomach, and like a light switch going off, he doesn't see anything else.

Chapter Thirty-Five

Oren has his arms around me.

I feel warm and cozy, and there's nowhere else I would rather be. Oren's sleeping quietly, and his soft breathing is such an adorable sound. He seems so at peace.

I can't really sleep. At first I thought it was because I was a little cold, so I put my boxers and T-shirt back on. That didn't help, so now I know it's just my anxious self going into overdrive, because Eli has been captured and it's all over, but I can't get my mind to relax.

I wish I could get my brain to shut up. Here I am, in bed with the guy I like, and everything should be perfect. I should be living the life that I longed for, all those years after Lake Priest. Things are even better with Mikey and Alyson. The nightmare is over.

Yet I can't sleep.

I hear something. It's faint, only just audible. At first I think I'm imagining it, but I roll over, just to check.

The door handle is turning. Someone is picking the lock.

"Oren," I say, my voice thick with fear. "Oren . . ."

The door opens as he wakes up.

The Freak is standing in the doorway, holding a knife. He rushes forward, his knife lifted up above his head. I jump out of the bed and fall down onto the floor. I stumble forward, crashing into the TV and knocking it over. Oren wakes and lets out a yelp. My Taser. I left it in the pocket of my jeans. I see them and wonder if I could get there in time.

From the bed, Oren reaches out and jams a Taser into the Freak's side. The Freak spasms and collapses onto the coffee table. Oren gets out of bed, dressed only in an old T-shirt and boxers. We sprint out of the room.

"How?" asks Oren.

"I don't know."

We run down the hall, and I stop. Why are we running? Oren hit him with the Taser. He must've remembered it once I was asleep. If we can trap him in the room, then we can just wait until the cops get here.

"What are you doing?" asks Oren.

"Finishing this."

I run back to the room and grab the door handle to close it. The door bursts open, hitting me in the nose, knocking me to the floor. I raise a hand to protect my head as there's a flash of silver; it feels like something red hot has burned my arm. I see my forearm has a deep gash. Blood jets from it, spraying everywhere. Fuck. He hit an artery maybe.

The Freak looks down at me.

Oren charges the Freak and tackles him. They hit the ground and start to wrestle.

"Run!" shouts Oren.

I get up and watch the wrestling pair. Oren punches the Freak, then pushes up off him, pulling me out of my shock. Oren and I run to the steps.

I reach the stairs, and a hand shoves me in the back, and I trip. I brace myself, then hit the stairs and start tumbling over and over. I can't control it—I'm going too fast. I reach the bottom of the stairwell and roll to a stop. My head is foggy, and my ears are ringing. I can faintly hear Oren crying my name as someone takes hold of my arms and pulls me up.

My head clears, and I see the Freak slowly coming down the stairwell, running his knife along the railing. Oren tries the front door, but it's locked. A key has been jammed in the lock, and the end has been snapped off, making the door useless.

"What do you want?" I cry.

"We split up on three," whispers Oren. "He'll chase me, you get help. You go left, I go right."

I don't want to, but my head is still so foggy, and I can't think of any other plan.

"Now."

Oren and I split up, with him running to the right. I go left, which leads to the meeting room with the pool table.

As I run, I see Oren was wrong. The Freak is chasing me.

"Why are you fighting?" says the Freak. "You must know you deserve this."

I grab a pool cue from the wall and hold it. The Freak lifts his knife.

"You never know when to give up, do you?"

"It's not my thing."

The Freak advances. I turn the pool cue and aim it like a poker. I jab as hard as I can, and I catch the Freak in the throat. He makes a choking sound, and I run past him, through the house, to the back door. I sprint outside and see Oren is in the backyard. I slam the door behind me, then take one of the outdoor chairs and wedge it against the door handle.

There, he's trapped.

I turn to Oren, expecting to see him impressed. But he's not. His mouth is stretched and drawn back.

"Sam, your arm."

I look down, and it's a brilliant red.

I stagger, and my back hits the wall. I try to plant my feet, but they aren't strong enough, and I feel myself falling, until a pair of strong hands grabs me by the waist and lowers me to the ground. Oren. He moves away, assessing the situation.

Pain slams into me. I turn my left arm, where the scar is. There's a long slash, deep enough to show red flesh underneath, glistening with blood. Everywhere below the cut is red, and it's rubbed off on my clothes, and my head is starting to feel light and dreamy. Not a good sign. Nor is Oren's expression, his face flushed and his eyes wide. I get it. There's way too much blood. Now that everything has slowed down, the pain comes in even stronger, as if my wrist is wrapped in a live-wire. I start to hyperventilate.

I'm dying. I . . .

There's a blur of movement, and then Oren presses some material over the wound. I can just make out his blurry outline, including his bare shoulders. He pushes his shirt onto the wound, and the pain becomes white-hot. It feels like sharp teeth have bitten into my forearm and are trying to sever my arm from my body, pulling at the tendons and muscle, stretching them until they start to snap.

"Hey," says Oren, his voice bringing me back just enough for my vision to clear. "Stay with me."

I look past Oren to the backyard of the house. It hasn't been cleaned from the party yet, so it's a mess, with bottles and cans strewn across the lawn. The inflatable pool has been trampled, and the water inside is murky. I fixate on it as the brightest thing in my field of vision. Another question looms over it all: How? Eli was the killer, and Oren and the rest of the brothers caught him. How can this be happening?

I close my eyes and lean my head against the wall. It'd be so easy to just slip into the dark right now.

"Sam!"

Oren grabs my cheeks and makes me look up at him, pulling me back once more. As soon as he lets me go, my head lulls back; I'm not strong enough to stop it.

"My friend, he's been attacked," says Oren, his voice just breaking through the fog. "He's losing a lot of blood, I think he's going to pass out. He . . ."

It comes on really fast, and I realize I'm going to faint, I can't stop it.

Everything goes white.

Chapter Thirty-Six

Something is beeping over and over.

I gingerly open my eyes. I'm in a dimly lit hospital room, lying on an uncomfortable bed. Through a window is a view of the night sky. Oren is slumped down in a chair on the other side of the room, his head against the top of the backrest. I try to sit up, but I feel a surge of pain in my arm. Last night, or what I think was last night, comes back to me.

The Freak tried to kill us.

There are tubes stuck into my wrist, and my injured forearm is covered in bandages, but there isn't any pain, now that I'm still.

"Oren," I say. My throat is dry and scratchy.

He sits up. "Hey, how are you feeling?"

"Not great."

"I have to tell you something," says Oren. "A few people were attacked last night."

Tears appear in his eyes.

"Who?" I ask.

"Josh is gone. He stabbed Mikey and Beth, but they're

alive, at least for now. Mikey's in surgery; they say it's touch-and-go."

I can't process it. Josh is dead. Mikey and Beth are both in the hospital. The nightmare was supposed to be over, and now this has happened.

"Is Eli still in custody?"

"He is."

My instincts were right. Eli isn't the killer. He can't be. I had one moment where I thought everything was okay, where I could be happy. But I was wrong. It's not over.

I go to pull the tubes out of my wrist, but Oren gets up and puts his hands on top of mine, stopping me.

"You need to rest," says Oren.

"He's still out there. He killed Josh. I . . ."

A nurse walks into the room and scowls at Oren. He retreats, moving back to his chair on the other side of the room. The nurse presses a cold, clammy hand to my forehead, and I have to fight the urge to shake my head to get her hand off me.

"You have to let me go," I say.

She picks up a needle and flicks it twice.

"What are you doing?"

I try to move as far away as I can, but the tubes hold me in place. She moves quickly and injects me with the needle.

"It's just a sedative," says the nurse. "To calm you down. You need to heal."

No.

I become very tired, but I know I can't pass out. A killer is still out there, and he'll be coming after me, to finish the job. If I'm unconscious, I'm completely helpless.

"Don't worry," says the nurse. "Your family will be here soon."

"No," I say, my speech slurred. "Oren, don't let them!"

"Shh. Rest."

My head becomes very heavy, and my body starts to sink into the mattress. I fight it as much as I can, but I'm not strong enough, and the darkness takes hold.

I'm going to drown.

I'm on a small sailboat, surrounded by endless ocean in the midst of the biggest storm I've ever seen. The sky crackles with lightning, and the rain is so thick I can barely see. My clothes are soaking wet, weighing me down.

I grab hold of the mast and use it to pull myself to my feet. I'm going to fight until the very last second, with every ounce of willpower that I have. My eyes sting. I wince, unable to believe what I'm seeing.

A towering wave is coming toward me. It's so tall I have to tilt my head back in order to see all of it. It's a solid, moving wall of dark water, foaming at the top, casting a long shadow. The air grows cold, and time seems to slow as my world grows dim. There's nowhere for me to run, no way for me to escape.

I cling on tight to the mast.

Here we go.

The wave reaches me, and the boat starts to climb. It moves upward at high speed, so fast that my grip on the slippery mast starts to falter. Salt water sprays onto my face, and I can taste it on my lips. I'm not going to let go. I can't.

I reach the top of the wave, and I'm nearly horizontal, and the only thing stopping me from plummeting to my death is my grip. I scream, the noise barely audible over the roar of the storm. The boat reaches the top, cresting over the lip.

"Sam," says a distant voice. *Oren. "Your family is here."*

Wait.

This isn't real. It's a nightmare.

I need to wake up. I run across the boat, my shoes slapping against the wet floor. This is a dream; the only way to escape it is to die. I find the anchor and pick it up, then move over to the side of the boat. The water is a deep blue, almost black. I get up onto the edge of the boat, grab the anchor, and jump into the water.

I sink straight down. Pressure around me builds. I open my eyes, even though all I can see is endless blackness. I feel tiny compared to everything around me. My lungs scream for air, and the pressure pushing on me becomes so intense I'm worried my head will burst. But I hold on to the anchor. I open my mouth, and water floods in. Watching me is a gargantuan Freak. His mouth opens wide to swallow me.

I wake up, and I feel the side of my face resting against a cool pillow. It worked. I glance around the room. I'm back in a hospital room, in a thin hospital gown. Out through a window I can see the night sky. The lights in the room off, and I'm alone. Then a feeling comes over me, as sure as anything. It's dread, starting from a place behind my stomach, then spreading out with long, thin fingers.

He's here.

I don't know how, or where, but I know it with everything I have. The feeling is overwhelming, and I'm sure I'm right. Pure evil is in this room with me. The door of the hospital room is wide open, letting in some yellow light from the hallway outside.

"Hello?" I call.

Silence. It was a long shot, anyway. There's nobody here, nobody who can help me. I glance down and see the device on the side of my bed. I grab it and press the assistance button, but my eyes don't dare leave the door.

The long shadow of a figure cuts through the light coming into the room. It draws closer, getting bigger and bigger, and I have to force myself to not look away, even if my whole body has seized up in fear. I blink and he's there, standing in the doorway, in his mask and his black leather jacket. He watches me, the wicked grin on his mask curving up to his ears.

He sprints forward, then leaps onto my bed. I kick at him,

but I'm weak and the hits bounce off him, useless. His knees dig into my chest as his bare hands wrap around my neck, his jagged fingernails scratching my skin. I feel his cold, sweat-slicked palms against my neck as he starts to squeeze. I reach up and feel the hard, shiny plastic of his mask. I feel it, searching for something where I can dig my fingers in, and then I reach the edge of his chin. I grab it and pull away, yanking the mask over his head.

My mind spins. It's Oren.

His expression doesn't change now that his identity has come into the light. His features are emotionless, totally plain, like he doesn't have his hands around my neck and is trying to squeeze the life out of me. His eyes are dead, totally dull. Unlike his mask, he isn't smiling. There's no humanity there. Just true evil, to his core. He squeezes harder.

I sit up, gasping.

I'm back in the hospital room. I pinch my arm, and it hurts. This is real. I am actually awake now.

Oren is still in the chair opposite me, dozing.

"Help," I say, waking him. "We need to go."

I grip the needle and pull it out of my hand. It hurts like hell, but I get it out. A single bead of blood wells up. I get out of bed and try to stand, but I collapse.

Oren catches me.

"Easy," he says.

"Where's my family?"

"They're in the waiting room. The doctor isn't letting anyone else see you until you're awake."

"Take me to them."

"I don't think that's a good idea."

"Please, I need to see them. They're not safe here."

"Okay. Here, let me help you."

We reposition ourselves so Oren is supporting most of my weight, and we go out into the hospital hallway. It's brightly lit and smells of antiseptic. Energy is slowly returning to my body, but still not enough to move properly. We reach the end of the hall and go out through a set of bright blue double doors.

The waiting room is quiet, the only sound coming from a few nurses down by a vending machine making hushed conversation. An ancient TV is on the wall, turned off at the moment. Mom and Peter are sitting together. They're facing a set of steel elevators. Fukuda is sitting in the corner of the room, watching.

Wait. Dad and Gus.

Where's Dad and Gus?

"Sam!" says Peter, leaping up and out of his seat. "What are you doing?"

"Where's Dad and Gus?"

"They're supposed to be with you," he says, his brows furrowing. "A nurse took them; he said—"

"What did he look like?"

"Um, he had brown hair, a beard, I think. He said he'd take them to you, that we could only visit one at a time. I didn't think . . . Oh God."

There's only one person I know who has brown hair and a beard. There's only one person who makes sense.

Booker.

Someone screams. I turn and see Dad emerge from the hallway, clutching his stomach. Blood pumps out from between his fingers, dropping to the hospital floor.

"Gus," he says. "He has Gus."

He collapses.

Chapter Thirty-Seven

I can't panic.

I want to. I want to scream and cry, or shut down out of pure fear, but I can't. Booker—the Freak—has Gus, and I have no doubt he will kill him. Even though he's just a kid, he isn't safe, not from him. Booker stabbed Dad and took my brother. I'm nearly sick, bile surging up my windpipe, and I only just manage to keep it down. Every second counts right now, because he has my little brother. He has *Gus*.

A nurse has rushed to Dad's side and is applying pressure to his wound. I can't do anything to help him, but Gus needs me.

"Where's my phone?" I ask, the desperation clear in my voice.

"Back in the room," says Oren.

Fukuda gets up and comes over.

"What's wrong?" she asks.

"Get security," I say to Fukuda as I start making my way back toward my room. "I think Booker, the nurse, is the Freak and he has my brother. Find him!"

Fukuda rushes toward a hallway with Mom trailing behind her. Fukuda runs to the desk. Dad is lifted onto a stretcher. I want to go to him, but I know I can't. I turn and go back to my room, trying my best to sprint. I can't run, because of the drugs still coursing through my veins, but I go as fast as I can. Oren pushes open the double doors for me, leading to a long corridor.

"Sam," says Oren, "you're bleeding."

He's right, I can feel it: The stitches have pulled loose, and now my arm is getting soaked with blood. I don't care. Not while Gus is in danger. I make it back to my room and find my clothes in a pile on the chair in the corner. I reach for them, but pain cripples me. I lean one hand against the wall and breathe, hoping the pain will die down. The room offers a few places for a killer to hide. He could be crouching behind the bed, or behind the curtains. The pain isn't fading, but I'm getting used to it. I push up off the wall, then lift my jeans and pull my phone out of the pocket. Face ID works, and my phone unlocks. The energy bar is in the red. I swipe through and call the last number used to taunt me. I thought it was Eli, but now I know I was wrong. It was Booker. I call Eli's number, which I now know Booker has been controlling this whole time. Eli's story must be true; it's the only thing that makes sense.

The call connects.

"Hello, Sam."

"Where's Gus?"

"He's here with me. Say hello."

"Sam!" shouts Gus.

"Shh," he says, cutting him off. "We're on the sixth floor, room six thirty-four. If I see any security or police I'll slit his throat, but you can save him. Bring your boyfriend if you want, but nobody else. You have five minutes."

He hangs up.

I start typing a message to Fukuda. My hands are shaking too much, and blood smears onto the screen, making my words come out incomprehensible. I wipe my hand on a clean part of my gown, smearing it with blood, then start typing again. This time, I manage to get it right, and I finish the message but don't send it. I want a head start.

Clutching my phone, I run back out.

The lights in the hospital turn off, and a loud siren starts to wail. Around us, doctors, nurses, and patients stop what they were doing, puzzled.

Oren and I make our way down the hall.

"Did he message?" he asks.

"He's on the sixth floor, with Gus."

"We need to tell security," he says.

"We can't."

"Why?"

"He'll kill him if he sees them. I need to get there first, to—*Ah*."

I grimace, as the pain from my arm grows unbearable. It

feels like it's been put in a wood chipper. I start to get lightheaded and have to fight back the urge to faint. The siren continues to wail, loud and piercing. I bang into the wall, and the black clouds creep in.

"You need help," says Oren.

He's right. Blood is dripping even through the bandages now, and I'm not sure I have much left to lose.

"He's my brother," I say. "I have to."

"Okay, then. Let's go."

We reach the end of the hallway and find there's a large crowd formed around the elevators.

"The stairs," says Oren.

We run to them, skirting around the crowd, and then go into the stairwell. We're on level three now. I look up at the long stretch of stairs above me. I take the first step up, and I fall, just managing to catch myself with my good hand before my face lands on a concrete stair.

"Sam!" says Oren. "Oh fuck."

I see it, too. I can barely move, and blood is pumping from my arm. I can smell it, too, like rust. I think I'm dying. I push myself up, but I'm too weak, and I collapse again.

"Help me," I say. "It's not far."

Oren doesn't move.

I grimace, and try to push through the pain. It's overwhelming, but I need to be stronger. "Please. I can save him. Please."

"What about you, Sam?"

"I'll be fine. Help me."

Oren rushes forward and slings my arm over his shoulder. With him supporting me, I can stand.

"You better not die on me," he says.

"I don't plan on it."

We climb up the stairs, making it to the fourth level. Oren is supporting most of my weight, but he's not showing any signs of giving up. Okay. Two to go. We make it to the fifth level. And then the sixth. Oren's puffing and panting, and the pain is so bad now, but we make it.

The sixth-floor hallway is empty and dark. The siren continues to wail, the same shrill alarm over and over. An old man in a robe is standing in his doorway, clearly confused. He rocks back and forth, his toothless mouth opening and closing, making a low confused moan.

We go past him. His room is 627, and the next is 628, so we're going in the right direction. I cling on to Oren's shirt. If we can make it there in time . . . We reach the door to room 634, and Oren opens it.

"Wait," I say.

I send the message to Fukuda. I'd guess that gives me a few minutes until she can get here. I need to get Gus away from Booker before the officer makes it.

It's one of the luxury suites, so it's spacious; one of the

walls is a huge window. The Freak is at the back of the room, holding a knife to Gus's throat.

"You made it," says the Freak.

"Get away from my brother," I say.

"No."

Oren steps closer, and the Freak presses the knife against Gus's throat, stopping Oren.

"Easy, beefcake," says the Freak. "Come here, and get on your knees."

Oren hesitates.

"*NOW!*" screams the Freak.

Oren walks away from me and gets on his knees.

"Hands behind your head," says the Freak.

Oren does as he's told. Fuck. I need a plan, but I can't think of anything. There's not much I can do while Booker has his knife to Gus's throat. If we make one mistake, then his throat will be slit.

My plan. I told Fukuda where we are, and she'll be on her way, with a gun. She can't be far away. That's the only chance I have. I need to stall until she can get here and put a bullet in his skull. Clouds of black swirl around my vision. The Freak snaps his fingers, pushing the darkness back.

"Why are you doing this?" I ask.

"You killed my brother, Sam. So I'm going to kill yours."

With his free hand, he pulls off his mask. I was right, it's Booker.

"Nobody ever suspects the stoner, do they?" he asks. "It was so perfect! Just smell like weed and nobody even *thinks* you could be the killer. It was so easy."

"You're sick," I spit.

"No, you are!" screams Booker. "My brother raised me. He was brilliant, and funny. And you killed him. And then, was there a trial? No. Everybody wanted him to be dead, so everyone forgot he was a person. But I didn't. If they wouldn't make you pay, then I would."

I glance down and see Gus reaching toward his pocket. His Taser. Does he have it?

"I'm going to give a choice of punishment, Sam," says Booker. "I will kill Gus or your boyfriend. You have five seconds, or I'll kill them both."

I can't do this.

"Choose, now."

He grabs Oren by the hair, pulling him closer.

"Sam, pick me," says Oren. "I forgive you."

"Booker," I say. "Please stop. I did it, okay. I killed Shawn, and I'm sorry. Kill me, but don't hurt them."

"Time's up," says Booker.

Gus turns his Taser toward Booker and jams it into his leg. Booker spasms and drops the knife. Gus runs forward, into my arms. On the ground, Booker continues to shake.

He threatened Gus. He was going to kill him.

I go forward, until I reach Booker's dropped knife. He

has killed so many people with this knife. Justin. Brian. Tripp. Josh. McDougall.

I bend down and pick up the knife.

"Sam," says Oren. "What are you doing?"

"Do it," spits Booker. "You know you want to."

I pick up the knife. It would be so easy; he's helpless right now. I could plunge it into his chest. Nobody would blame me. After everything he's done, after all the lives that he's taken and all the lives that he's changed forever in his quest for vengeance, is it fair that he gets to live?

No.

This isn't me. I'm not a killer.

I toss the knife away.

The door swings open, and Fukuda bursts in with a squadron of security guards.

"He's all yours," I say.

Chapter Thirty-Eight

Everything is too bright.

Everything is white and burns my eyes.

"Sam," says a familiar voice.

Mom.

She takes hold of my hand as my eyes adjust, and I become aware of my surroundings. I'm back in a hospital room, and it's clearly midday, as bright sunlight is coming in through the window. My arm has been freshly bandaged, and while I feel like shit, I'm alive. What happened comes back to me in a rush. Booker is the Freak. He had Gus, but Gus beat him.

It's over.

"Dad," I say.

"He's okay," she says. "Gus too."

Relief washes over me.

"Where are they?"

"They're in their own rooms. Gus has been awake all day, and—"

"How long have I been out?"

"Only a few hours. You lost a lot of blood. It was touch-and-go there for a while, but I knew you'd pull through. You're tough, kid."

"Where's Peter?"

"He's with Gus. I'll go get him, but there's something I want to tell you first." Mom tears up.

I wasn't actually sure she could cry, I don't think I've ever seen it.

"I've asked my publisher to pull *The Pleasant House*."

It has to be the drugs talking. There's no way she said what she just did. Not now, when sales and interest would be higher than they've ever been.

"I could've lost both of you," she says. "I'll write my own story. Yours should belong to you." She wipes her eyes. "I do have a new idea. It's a romance. Maybe you could critique it for me one day."

"I'd like that."

She pats me on the hand, then gets up and leaves. A few minutes later she returns with Peter. He rushes into the room and stops at my bedside.

"How are you feeling?" asks Peter.

Like I've been stabbed.

"Sore," I say.

"We could get you some more painkillers if you'd like?"

"I'm okay; thanks, Peter." I sit up so I'm more comfortable. "How's Gus?"

"He asked if this means he can get a PlayStation."

I almost laugh. "Of course he did."

"He's putting on a brave front," says Peter. "But he'll be okay. And if he's not, we'll be there for him."

"We all will," says Mom.

That's what Mom and Peter seem like right now. A united front.

"I heard you're awake."

Oren is standing in my hospital doorway. Even all the drugs in me right now can't stop the intense rush of endorphins I get at just the sight of him.

"We'll give you two a minute," says Peter, then whispers before the three of them leave, "Good luck."

Oren comes in, taking their place.

"I'm sorry," I say. "I dragged you into all of this."

"Don't be sorry. None of that was your fault. And it's my choice. And where I want to be is with you. If you want that."

"I do."

He smiles, and taps his hands on the railing of my bed.

"So," he says. "How about that date?"

Epilogue

A thump sounds on Sam's door, startling him.

He smiles, gets up from his desk, and trudges over to his door. Sunlight is bright gold outside, lighting up his dorm room. His hair is long enough to tussle, and he is tanned and healthy. There's a lacrosse stick leaning against the wall, and the sneakers he wears while playing are under his bed. He reaches the door, then stops for a moment, eyeing the Taser that he has on his desk within easy reach. He ignores it and opens the door. A part of him still thinks that a nightmare might be outside. The Freak, or some other masked killer, is waiting for him. But that thought is distant now and easy to ignore as long as he works at it.

Oren is standing outside, his hands shoved into his pockets. He thrusts his hands into the air, uncharacteristically animated. "Spring break, baby!"

Sam grabs Oren by the shirt and pulls him into his room. The pair totter backward, and Oren pushes Sam's door closed. Sam leans forward and kisses his boyfriend.

"Well, hello to you, too," says Oren.

Sam goes to kiss him, but Oren turns his head, his focus landing on the open, and only half-packed, suitcase on Sam's bed. Oren lifts an eyebrow.

"I got distracted writing," says Sam.

This has been happening lately, more often than not. After he got out of the hospital, he changed majors to creative writing, and, given how well he is doing in his classes and how happy he is, he knows it was the right decision. Sam goes over to his laptop, closes it, then quickly finishes packing.

"You know we leave in five minutes, right?" asks Oren.

"One more," asks Sam.

Oren gives it to him. And then another one for good measure.

A few kisses later, Sam and Oren go downstairs, where the rest of the AΦN brothers are piled into a van. Jerome hops out of the driver's seat and comes over to hug Sam. Jerome has been excelling in his role as president, and even though this stretch of time will be remembered as one of the darkest in the brotherhood's history, he has made sure that the brothers have remained close.

The drive passes quickly, and soon, they're all checked in at the airport and walking to the gate. As Sam collects his boarding pass, he notices Alyson, in a bright floral dress.

Ever since he got back from the hospital, the pair have started hanging out all the time again.

An hour later, Sam is sitting between Oren and Alyson on a plane filled with other spring breakers. Everyone seems to be wearing the loudest outfit they own, so the plane is kind of a Technicolor nightmare. A group of sorority girls start blasting Sean Paul's "Temperature" from a set of portable speakers, and people start singing along. Sam joins in, surprising Alyson.

"You know the words?" she asks.

"You don't?"

"I mean, I do, but I'm not going to sing it."

"You've just got to lean into it."

What can he say? He is going to spring break, and he is sitting next to his best friend and his boyfriend. Life is good.

A flight attendant hurries toward them and tells them to shut off the music.

"Devastating," says Alyson.

Sam laughs.

Farther down the plane, Mikey and his new boyfriend, a guy named Zamir, are holding hands. Even if they had a rough start, now Sam truly considers Mikey his brother. Farther forward is Beth. Given her level of fame, he's surprised she's coming to this.

"Spring break!" shouts someone, and the crowd cheers.

The hotel that Jerome booked is about as Florida as it gets.

It has bright pink walls, and there's so much color everywhere. Workers in white shirts with deep tans and unnaturally perfect teeth stand behind the desk. There's a store in the corner of the lobby, which is selling spring break merch, including a tank top with SPRING BREAK FOREVER in big neon letters across the chest.

Sam, Oren, and Alyson go over to the store.

"You'd look good in that," says Oren.

That's all Sam needs to hear, so he grabs one in his size and buys it. As he leaves the store, he decides he should respond to the messages he got on the plane.

He responds to Mom first.

Have a good spring break, Sam. And stay safe.

I will!

Things between them still aren't fantastic; there's still a deep well of hurt there. But she's trying, and Sam appreciates that.

The next message is from Eli. After everything that happened, Eli decided he wanted to get away from Munroe, which is understandable. He and Sam message occasionally, and last Sam heard, Eli was in Chicago and had started a new band that was doing really well. They might not talk all the time, but Sam knows that if he ever needs him, Eli will be there. Sam hopes Eli feels the same way.

I heard it's spring break—have fun!!

Thanks!

He calls Dad.

"Sam!" he says, answering on camera. He's in the living room of Peter's house. He's obviously mustered Peter and Gus for this call.

"Look what I got!" says Sam, showing off his new tank.

Gus scrunches up his face.

"What?"

"It's so tacky."

"But that's the charm, right?" asks Sam.

"If you say so."

Sam scowls, outraged.

"What's the weather like there?" asks Peter.

"*Humid.*"

It really is. Sam is already starting to sweat.

"I'm going to swim," says Sam. "I'll call you later."

Sam ends the call. He goes out the lobby to the pool and spots Oren and Alyson sitting next to each other, sunbathing. Sam pulls his tank off and then drops down onto a deck chair next to Oren. Surrounding them is a swarm of spring breakers. Oren gives Sam a kiss in greeting.

Sam sits for a while, letting his mind grow blank. Oren gets up and walks toward the pool. Sam watches his boyfriend for a moment too long. Alyson catches him and lowers her sunglasses an inch.

"Shut up," he says.

Sam's phone chimes.

It's a message from an unknown number. They've taken a photo of him, obviously a few seconds ago, as Oren is no longer beside him. Sam searches the pool for who could've taken it, but there are hundreds of people here. A message comes in.

Ready to die, Sam?

Sam starts typing a message. Once he's written it, he smiles and starts planning his next move.

Good luck.

ACKNOWLEDGMENTS

A part of me can't believe I'm writing the acknowledgments of this book. Wild.

Here it goes.

First, I want to thank Nicholas. Thank you for being such an incredible, supportive boyfriend throughout this whole process. I love you.

To Liz Szabla and the entire team at Feiwel and Friends, including copyeditors Valerie Shea and Bonnie Cutler, and senior production editor Lelia Mander, thank you for your patience and support while I worked to get this book right. And to Xia Gordon for the brilliant, and super-creepy, cover! I love it so much. To Moe Ferrara, for being a dream agent for this even if it was a book you didn't sell, and for everything you've done for me this past year, and to Leon Husock for selling the book in the first place. To all, thank you so much.

Jayden! I dedicated this book to you because you're the most fun person to watch horror movies with, as well as being an incredible person I love so much. I hope this book gets a more positive reaction than a sarcastic "interesting."

Fingers crossed. Seriously, you're the best little brother a guy could hope for.

Mum, Dad, Kia, and Shaye . . . all icons. Thanks for always being there for me when I want to excitedly talk to you when something publishing related happens, and for everything else, too. Special shout-out to Kia for your amazing notes on this, and for making the "stabby-stab-stab" book the best possible version it could be.

To friends Sophie Gonzales, Becky Albertalli, Caleb Roehrig, Adam Sass, Adib Khorram, Julian Winters, Tom Ryan, Lev AC Rosen, Alex London, Tricia Levenseller, Shaun David Hutchinson, Rogier, Allaricia, and David Slayton: thank you, all, for everything. Special shout-out to Sophie, for the constant chats that always bring me so much joy. Callum McDonald came through once again with the editing notes—I hope you're happy with the description in the scene with Justin's teeth! To friends Jaymen, Raf, Mitch, Finella, Sarah, Asha, Lauren, Maddy, Dan, Ryan, Ross, Brandyn, and Kyle: thank you for being amazing!

And lastly, thank you to you, for reading this and for supporting me. Thank you so much!